NUGGETS

FIVE PLAYS

BERNARD GARDNER

iUniverse, Inc.
New York   Bloomington

Nuggets
Five Plays

iUniverse books may be ordered through booksellers or by contacting:

iUniverse
1663 Liberty Drive
Bloomington, IN 47403
www.iuniverse.com
1-800-Authors (1-800-288-4677)

ISBN: 978-1-4502-7468-5 (sc)
ISBN: 978-1-4502-7469-2 (ebook)

Printed in the United States of America

iUniverse rev. date: 12/10/2010

THE BLUE YONDER

AN ORIGINAL PLAY WRITTEN BY BERNARD GARDNER

"LOVER'S MOOD"
ORIGINAL MUSIC AND LYRICS BY

BERNARD GARDNER
AND
JOAN E. GARDNER

THE BLUE YONDER   CAST OF CHARACTERS.

IN ORDER OF APPEARANCE

NURSE MARNI SMITH   At the desk of AF Hospital Clinic
NURSE ROBERTA MATZ
LADY #1
LADY # 2   With carriages.
AIRMAN # 1
AIRMAN # 2
DOCTOR GEORGE ANDERSON (CAPTAIN GENERAL SURGEON)
DOCTOR HOWARD JAMESON (CAPTAIN GENERAL SURGEON)
DOCTOR ARTHUR HARRIS (MAJOR NEUROSURGEON)
DOCTOR ANDREW KORN (CAPTAIN NEUROLOGIST)
DOCTOR CHARLES DORRIN (CAPTAIN NEUROLOGIST)
DOCTOR ROBERT GORDON (MAJOR THORACIC SUGEON)
ANNE GETTES (SECRETARY)

DANCERS

DOCTOR   VINCENT   COMPAGNE   (COLONEL   HOSPITAL
COMMANDER)
CAPTAIN NORRIS (AIDE TO COMPAGNE)
DOCTOR   GEORGE   FITZHUGH   (CAPTAIN   CHIEF   OF
RADIOLOGY)

COMEDIAN
WAITER

MARGE ANDERSON
ANDREA DEXTER
DOCTOR PHILIP DEXTER (MAJOR CHIEF OF OB-GYN)
POLLY GORDON
ALICE JAMESON

COLONEL WALTER STANTON (INVESTIGATOR)

ACT I
SCENE 1

(The setting is an Air Force Base in the 1950s. This is an essentially peacetime military base although the cold war is at its height and the SAC units are maintaining planes in the air every minute of every day. This particular base is MATS - military air transport for goods and personnel to and from the far east and also the base from which air force officers seeking service related disabilities after 20 years of service are evaluated prior to discharge. The base is run by a combination of regular Air Force officers, those repaying 4 to 7 years of sponsored time, and 2-year conscripts. The latter two groups are mostly doctors. Since there are no hot wars there's a lot of spare time available.)

(As the curtain rises we are in the waiting room of a medical clinic. Upstage center is the intake desk manned by a nurse. Several chairs are lined up at either side. Downstage left are two chairs occupied by young ladies each with a pram or baby carriage which they rock intermittently.)

Lady #1:   Hi, I'm June Amallons. I don't believe we've met. How often do you come up here?

Lady #2 :   Oh at least once a week. It gives me something to do..... and I can usually   pick up some meds we ran out of. I don't mind getting examined.................. By now the Docs just have a prescription ready. My name is Mary Justine. My husband's an E3. ..Works over at the motor pool.

Lady #1:   Yeah!.... I need to get out once in awhile too. I don't mind comin here. I get a   pain sometimes............ the Doc's are pretty good........... they'll look at the baby

5

too............. Same visit. My husband works over at the warehouse.. He helps the Docs out sometimes.......... Got one of them an extra bed to use for company.. They mostly know me by now.

(An airman walks in, approaches the intake desk and starts to fill out the forms. The nurse picks them up and addresses the patient)

Nurse: What seems to be your problem?

Airman: I have a pain in my stomach.

Nurse: How long have you had it?

Airman: *(looking at his watch)* Well......... it looks going on twenty five minutes now.

Nurse: Well have a seat. The doctor will see you shortly.

Lady#1: Doesn't seem so crowded today.

Lady#2: Wait till tomorrow............. There's a march on base........... Four   miles..........Everyone 'll be in here looking for an excuse to get out of that.

Lady#1: Yeah That's right.

(An Airman limps on stage flexed and holding his buttock. He can barely move. He crawls over to the nurses' desk and hands her a slip He is followed by two doctors)

Nurse: Well it's back to duty for you young man. *(He crawls off stage)*

Doctor Anderson: I don't think you treated that abscess correctly! You're supposed to identify the internal fistula and excise it. After three days of sitz baths they're cured.

Doctor Jameson: Don't you think I know that? I've had good training. But you have to read Directive #351A - Treatment of rectal abscesses. " These shall be incised and drained and the patient referred back to regular duty." You can't put them in the hospital.

Doctor Anderson: Yeah! I guess it's welcome to Air Force medicine. ....This way the damn thing is guaranteed to recur.

Doctor Jameson: But they don't lose any time from duty.

(The waiting patient gets up stretches and starts to leave)

Patient: Well I guess I feel better now......... *(he runs off stage).*

Doctor Anderson: One less problem...By the way, What's with that psychiatrist Jones? He's paying me a hundred bucks to take his MOD call.

Doctor Jameson: He's afraid of sick patients. It's worth it to him...... otherwise it's PANIC TIME. You know the military............ as long as you've got an MD you can take care of anybody. They put that new OB-GYN in the path lab and they've got the new E level pathologist doing OB call.

Doctor Anderson: Speaking of sickos, How did that major Bart ever get through his surgical training. He doesn't even know how to hold a scalpel. He trained at the Mayo didn't he?

Doctor Jameson: They just wanted him to go into the Air Force. I understand they trained him with movies............... Gordon gave me the job of scrubbing on all his cases and keeping him out of trouble.

Nurse Smith: And what about our temporary leader Lt. Col Swenson? My orders are to load him with paperwork so he never has to see patients.

Nurse Matz: By the way we're closing the clinic early today. We have a Medical Evaluation Board meeting at 1300 Hours. You guys have a good lunch.

Nurse Smith: I'll tidy up................ You know the new Hospital Commander is arriving tomorrow. I hear he's a real tiger. Fitzhugh knows him from a previous assignment.,,,,,,,,,,,,,,,,,,,,,, Hear they had trouble.

Nurse Matz: Yeah a tiger ....with the women................. I heard he's got some influence in Washington. He's sent around as a trouble-shooter.

Nurse Smith: Been in plenty of trouble himself.

(The nurses set up the chairs for the board meeting leaving space for the patients to be seen. They all exit......... Lights off)

ACT I
SCENE 2

(The medical board filters on stage. It consists of neurosurgeon Captain Harris as the chairman, two neurologists Captains Korn and Dorrin, two nurses, general surgeon Captain Anderson, and Ob-Gyn Major Dexter. Secretary Anne Gettes handles the records and takes minutes.)

Doctor Harris: *(He turns to Korn and Dorrin who have arrived together)* Hey Welcome back you two. Had a month in Europe eh? All paid for with TDY pay. How'd you ever swing that?

Doctor Korn: You know Harris ....You just don't appreciate talent!

Doctor Harris: Yeah I'll bet................

Doctor Dorrin: Hope you didn't operate on anyone while we were gone.

Doctor Harris: Fat chance. You know if it was up to you two they'd close up the neurosurgical boards.

Doctor Korn: Amen to that thought.

Major Gordon: OK cut it out you guys.

Captain Harris: All in fun. Nobody takes New York Neurologists seriously any more.

Anne Gettes: I have all the records available. I typed out summaries for everyone.

Doctor Anderson: Annie you're a whiz. I've never met a secretary who can type 150 words a minute. Thanks for doing all my Or Notes.

Anne: Oh I love being helpful. Besides you guys take care of me and Jim when we need medical advice.

Captain Harris: We'd better get started. We don't want to miss Happy Hour.

Anderson: Harris How do you decide who gets considered for a disability?

Harris: It's easy. All these officers are retiring with Back Pain. Everybody has Back Pain ... and they know all the symptoms. I offer them a myelogram and if they're stupid enough to go through having dye injected into their spines they deserve a disability. We'll set the amounts now.

Korn: Sounds like typical neurosurgical thinking.

Major Gordon: Ok Annie have them come in.

(At this point all are seated and five officers file in. They are each in Pajamas, bent over and walking with a cane. They do a choreographed dance to the music of "Dem Bones" lasting about 2-3 minutes As their names are called each staggers over to the board in various degrees of pain. The board then votes by consulting and then holding up a sign with a number depending on the degree of disability. Numbers range from 10 to 40 and Anne announces the amount and records it. Each patient then straightens up and skips off stage.)

Harris: Well that wasn't too bad was it?

Anderson: No point in leaving before the bugle. The bar won't be open yet!

Korn: What have you guys heard about the new Hospital Commander?

Gordon: A real son of a bitch. Tough on everybody. Fitzhugh knows him from McCabe.

Dorrin: When do we get to meet him?

Gordon: He arrives tomorrow. He'll have everybody in by evening.

Nurse Smith: I assume the nurses will be included.

Nurse Matz: You can count on it.

Nurse Smith: I've seen his type before.

(They all jockey for positions at the door. Nurse Matz touches the arm of Gordon they look at each other and he moves away. The bugle sounds and they rush offstage except for Nurse Smith.. She takes out her lipstick and mirror primps a bit then walks slowly off stage. Lights out)

ACT II
SCENE 1

(Colonel Vincent Compagne is seated behind his desk . He is meeting with members of the hospital staff. Several non coms are standing before him)

Col. Compagne: I trust you all understand my position. People who wish to get along do not question any of my orders That's how I know they are my friends. I was sent here to get this hospital in shape and I will carry that out. Now one more thing......... Good grooming means polished shoes that reflect light like a mirror. I would strongly suggest that you keep shoe polish in your lockers and use it frequently. Now you are dismissed....................
(They leave)
Norris ......NORRIS...............Get in here when I call.

Captain Norris: Yes sir.

Compagne: Where have you been all morning?

Captain Norris: I'm on the Lawn Patrol today Sir. I was riding around reviewing lawns.

Compagne: Are you kidding? Let me see the citations......................There's only one?

Norris: Yes sir!

Compagne: 103 Waverly................. Why that's your address.

Norris: Yes sir!

Compagne: You gave yourself a ticket for not cutting your grass?

Norris: Yes sir!

Compagne: How did I end up with a crew of idiots?

Norris: Yes sir.

Compagne: Get out of here..............Send in Fitzhugh.

Norris: Yes sir:

(Captain George Fitzhugh enters, salutes, stands in front of the desk.)

Compagne: So we meet once again.

Fitshugh: Yes sir.

Compagne: Your tough luck George..... Let me see what stupid moves you've made lately. Did you order those manila envelopes mucking up the x-ray department?

Fitshugh: Yes............ I tried to streamline the department by using them to file our reports............. I ordered 2500.

Compagne: 2500?..................... Didn't you think central warehouse might be looking to unload these folders?..............get them off their hands.

Fishugh: No. I needed 1200 so I ordered 2500 figuring they'd send half like usual.
How did I know they'd ship 25,000.

Compagne: You're stupid. Now you can't navigate the department. There are cartons of these things in all the corridors. .... If they're not cleared by tomorrow they'll be dropped at your front door by Wednesday....................

Fitzhugh: I'm not stupid I resent your attitude........... Don't use that tone with me again.

Compagne: Or what? Your not built to take me on............

Fitzhugh: I don't need muscles to take you on..............

Compagne: Making any more problems?................Still have a loose tongue I see............... eh?....................As long I have this bird on my collar I'll use any tone I want and you'll stow it...............
    Dismissed........... Send Captain Norris in.

(He leaves and Norris enters)

Compagne: Norris call Battaglia in Washington get some orders cut reassigning Fitshugh..............Let's send him where he can't make any noise...................
    How about the Azores. ... Yes assign him to the hospital in the Azores. .

Norris: Yes sir. Korn and Dorrin are outside.

Compagne: Send those jokers in.

(Korn and Dorrin enter)

Compagne: At ease......... So you guys just came back from visiting every base in Europe eh? ....
    On TDY yet .... you got paid for your vacation...........

Together: Yes sir!

Compagne: Who the hell signed THOSE orders?

Korn: Base Commander General Johnson sir.

Compagne:	Yeah.......... I read the medical records.......... I see you treated him for a sinus headache................... after you worked him up for a brain tumor............
Dorrin:	Yes sir.
Compagne:	You spent three weeks and 70,000 dollars in work-ups for a sinus headache?
Korn:	We didn't want to miss anything...............
Compagne:	MISS ANYTHING?...............You injected air into his brain and dye into his ventricles for a condition you could treat with nose drops?...........
Dorrin:	He was very relieved to find out he didn't have a brain tumor.
Compagne:	I bet he was!............ So he sent you on a paid vacation! ...Pretty clever.. Ok you guys are on my list. Make one blunder and I'll have you on guard duty.
Korn:	We're out of the air force in 5 months............... You'll need us for the Medical Evaluation Board until we're replaced.
Compagne:	Yeah........Or I have to rely on that idiot neurosurgeon............What's his name........... Harris........... Okay you got away with one........... Dismissed.

(They leave)

Compagne:	Norris...........If Gordon is here send him in.

(Gordon enters, salutes and is at ease.)

Compagne:	I see you've spent some time in Africa. How'd you enjoy your station in the jungle?
Gordon:	I loved it. It gave me a chance to do some real surgery working with the special forces over there.
Compagne:	Yeah .... Got to know the natives............. I'd love to get back in the OR myself. I was a crackerjack..... Now they've used me to organize the hospitals in the system. I sit behind a desk. I get to work with assholes like Bart and Swenson. Keep them from killing anyone...........and dump the others to outlying post where they can't do much damage...............Major Gordon you're the best surgeon on base .... best I've seen in years..I'm counting on your support to see that everything runs smoothly......
Gordon:	Yes sir! I'll do my best.
Compagne:	I know you will............ You've still got seven years to go before you get your twenty in................ I know you won't give that retirement money up.
Gordon:	You're right about that.
Compagne:	Now what's this nonsense about operating on dogs?
Gordon:	Well we were under budget for several months. You know what that means........... They'd have cut the budget for the next period. So we spent the money on a dog lab and a heart-lung machine. We're investigating the effects of various drugs on the heart during open cardiac surgery...........Quite interesting.
Compagne:	Who's involved and who's taking care of the animals?

Gordon: Anderson is assisting me in the surgery. He's picking up techniques that are very helpful in the OR. Nurse Matz is giving the anesthesia and injecting the drugs. The equipment is excellent and we set up cages in the motor pool. The guys over there take care of the dogs. They get to keep the survivors.

Compagne: It doesn't sound like an activity that should be going on on base............. Nice to know where you and Anderson are spending your afternoons....................... Okay be careful. Dismissed.

Gordon: Yes sir. *(He turns and leaves.)*

Compagne: Norris anybody else?

Norris: Yes sir. Two of our nurses.

(Nurses Smith and Matz enter. They salute. Col. Compagne gets up and moves to the front of his desk. He looks them over carefully and directs them to stand straight, shoulders back, chest out.)

Compagne: Well.............. this is a pleasant ending to an otherwise horrible morning,

(Lights out)

ACT II
SCENE 2
(several months later)

(As the scene opens we are at the officer's club. Two tables are occupied. To the right are Major Gordon and hi wife Polly and Major Dexter and his wife Andrea. At the other table Captain Anderson is seated with his wife and Captain Jameson and his wife. A comedian is telling jokes which are having no effect on the groups. A piano is located upstage left.)

THREE JOKES

I.

Sam and Abe are riding the elevator down from their business in the garment center
Sam turns to Abe and says " My God! .... I think I left the SAFE open!"
Abe says: "SO WHAT ARE YOU WORRYING ABOUT.................. WE'RE BOTH HERE!

II.

A man walks into the Fountenbleu in Miami beach . He says: I VANT A SUITE ON THE EXECUTIVE FLOOR...................I'M A VURRY RICH MAN.
They get him a suite. He calls down to the desk: IT'S NOISY UP HERE. I'LL TAKE THE WHOLE FLOOR...................I'M A VURRY RICH MAN.
They clear the floor ....move everybody out.
He calls down to the desk: I'M GOING UP TO THE

SOLARIUM.............I WANT QUIET................I'M A VURRY RICH MAN.................
They ask everyone to leave the solarium. ....WHILE RELAXING ON THE CHEZ BE WARMED BY THE SUN ....HE LOOKS UP AT THE SKY ....OY HE SAYS..........WHO NEEDS MONEY?

III.

A man is sitting on a bench in Miami Beach A woman approaches him. She says:"YOU BUYING
....................I'M SELLING
They have a good time in a nearby hotel. When he gets back to New York he comes down with every transmitted disease known to man. He gets medicines, treatments, salves ....everything.
Exhausted he goes back the next year to Miami Beach to recuperate, He's sitting on the same bench when the same woman comes up to him.
SHE SAYS : "YOU BUYING.............I'M SELLING.
He looks at her and says WHAT'RE YOU SELLING THIS TIME?.................LEPROSY??

(As the performer leaves he's making nasty remarks about his agent booking him into this place....................Marge moves to the microphone and sings "Lover's Mood" accompanied on the piano.)

VERSE

When worldly woes surround
And flowers bend their heads
Cold and lonely nights abound
And frost will chill my bed

Your face my eyes caressed
Warms all the depths of my mind
To know with you I'm blessed
With love returned, two hearts combined

(*song:*   *LOVER'S MOOD*

My dream's complete when you are close to me
My hope's fulfilled for all eternity
Our love is a treasure
Words cannot measure
What my lips have tried in vain to say.

Sweetheart the moments you are here with me
Have made my life, my heart so gay and free
Our souls will surrender
Mem'ries that render
Many days of happiness not far away.)

(She finishes her song and sits. The conversation at each table can be heard
by the audience but not by the other table.)

Andrea:	I wonder who that song was intended for.
Polly:	I'm sure it wasn't old hubby.
Gordon:	You think she's been playing around?
Andrea:	Hear tell............ I think she'd trade her Captain for a Colonel.
Polly:	Waiter! Bring me another Tiger........ Where'd they dig up that comedian?
Dexter:	Yeah ...Awful........Why didn't they get some real Country music?
Polly:	Dahling.....You mean the music of single entendre?
Dexter:	Yeah... "I woke up in the morning....My gal left me ....I beat her up last night................ Don't she know I love her." .... Doesn't require an interpreter

(Polly is served another drink)

Gordon: Take it easy Polly.

Polly: I am................ I'm taking it as easy as I can get it

Dexter: What kind of poison you drinking?

Polly: It's green creme de menthe and vodka on ice........ mostly vodka. Try it you might like it.

Dexter: *(He takes a sip)* Not bad.

Gordon: It hits you later. It's a slow poison.... I prefer the rapid kind...........Waiter get me another scotch............ Are you still taking doubles on OB call?

Dexter: Yes. They assigned a pathologist to help out.. I'm trying to get Compagne to switch Goldberg over to me. At least he's got a year of OB training under his belt. The colonel's a bitch to deal with. ....He threatened to ship me out if I didn't toe the line with all of his directives.

Polly: Air Force Medicine...... They took Bob away from the states for a year. He had to live in Africa. .... We could be living in Malibu by now if we didn't have to pay all those training years back.

Gordon: But we do. I couldn't get through a residency without the Air Force salary...............You're not having such a bad time........ *(he takes her hand)*

Polly: I'm bored to death...Waiter *(she hands her glass to the waiter and gets a refill)*.

Andrea: How does Anderson stand it.

Gordon: He's one of the best we've had. I'd hate to imagine that while he's scrubbed..... his wife..............

Polly: This is getting maudlin. Let's talk about something besides Campagne..........Phil why do you eat at the club so often?

Dexter: Well ....It's a guarantee against constipation.

Andrea: Oh puleeze...........

(The spot switches to the other table. During the conversation the two nurses walk by accompanied by two male officers)

Anderson: You sang that beautifully,,,Hope you meant it for me.

Marge: Now who else would I mean it for.

Jameson: Great number. Now let's have a few drinks.. Waiter..............How about a bottle of wine? *(They all agree)*

Alice: As long as it's not I TAL IANNE.

Anderson: Please let's try not to mention the colonel. We have enough of him every day. He didn't can anyone today..That's a relief. Fitzhugh is leaving for the Azores at the end of the month.

Alice: Well whatever their argument was it apparently didn't involve his wife..............or the Colonel would have let him stay.

Anderson: Why what have you heard?

Jameson: George grow up. The rumors have been flying for weeks. He gets around quite a bit.

Marge: What rumors .... What are they saying?

Alice:	You know................. Oh please let's talk about something else.

Alice: You know................. Oh please let's talk about something else.

Marge: No................. What rumors?..............

Alice: Well Norris has been making his lawn rounds and apparently the colonel's car is showing up at a few strange places.

Jameson: Alice don't start spreading rumors. They could cause a lot of heartache........and may not be true............. George did you ever get your door taken down? The one that's blocking the entrance to your kitchen?

Anderson: You won't believe this. I put in a year ago to have the thing taken down and about six months ago some airman shows up and looks the door up and down.................... I thought he came to take it down but he said he was just evaluating it for the committee to report on how many man-hours it would take to take it off.

Jameson: Your kidding.......It's just a standard door. They can't figure that out without a committee meeting?

Anderson: Apparently not. Last week another airman came with a tape measure and started measuring the door. I asked if he was there to take it off. He said no............ he was just there to estimate the space it would take to store it in the warehouse... and report back to the committee.................................. We're gonna be here another six months and we're out. I know they'll take the door off and the next guy that moves into the house will want it put back on............... Good luck to him!

(They raise their glasses and drink except Marge who knocks the glass over. Lights out)

ACT II
SCENE 3

(A few days later. We are back in Colonel Compagne's office. He sits alone with a dim light. Norris enters with a Pizza box.)

Norris: I have your dinner Colonel. It was on my desk when I came in. . I'll be signing out, sir.

(He places the box on the desk, salutes and leaves. Colonel Compagne opens the box. He withdraws his hand quickly and shakes it and sucks it in his mouth. He curses something about the box being stapled. He looks the box over and takes a slice of pizza and eats it. He continues to work and after a few moments reaches for the box...looks it over and pushes it away...He grabs his throat and stands up, slowly reels and loses his footing and drops to the ground on one knee. He turns and writhes and passes out. Lights out.)

ACT III
Scene 1 (One week later)

(The scene is set up to reveal a living room with comfortable chairs and a couch. The entrance to the house will be stage right. Each of the actors will be on stage separately as the investigator conducts his interview. He is by turns ushered into the room and they are seated. He visits Major Dexter and Andrea.)

Col. Stanton: Hello. I'm Colonel William Stanton. I'm with the JAG in Washington sent here to investigate the facts in Colonel Compagne's demise. He was buried in Washington in a simple ceremony.

Dexter: Why'd they rush his body off base so quickly? We have pathologists here who could have done the autopsy.

Stanton: Not forensic pathologists. We also needed accurate toxicology. He died a few days after we got him. Never recovered consciousness.

Andrea: Horrible. What do think happened? Was he poisoned?

Stanton: We're still working out the details.

Dexter: Do you think he was killed by someone on this base? Did he have any evidence of an underlying medical problem?

Stanton: No he was in good health. I think it's probably certain that someone on this base did it. Do you know Dr. Fitzhugh? I believe they served together before. There was some bad blood between them.

Dexter: He's a mild mannered radiologist. He never even loses his temper.

Andrea: I know that the Colonel was having him transferred to the Azores. But He's never caused any trouble. His wife is a sweetheart.

Stanton: I guess he works with chemicals in the x-ray department..... Speaking of wives............ Colonel Compagne had a reputation ....

Dexter: We don't know anything about that! ,,,,,,,,,,,, Rumors are always being spread around on this base.

Stanton: Well it appears that Captain Norris was keeping a log of the Colonel's travels around the base. He didn't stop here but may have visited several of your friends................

Andrea: We don't know anything about such rumors.

Dexter: The only problem I had was his assignments of OBs to my service.

Andrea: Oh be quiet! Nobody would kill because of that!

Stanton: I understand that you both did some missionary work in New Guinea. Very commendable. ...... Why'd you go into medicine rather than the clergy?.........

Dexter: Yes we were with the church ministry..........We felt we could do more good working with people's problems instead of creating new ones.

Andrea: Phil......... Don't be so critical.......... We never wanted those natives to abandon their customs and society totally.............We actually made some close ties to the people who lived on the island. Their lives were orderly and peaceful before the plantation owners moved in and tried to make them over. .... When the air force offered to send us through medical school and training we decided it might be a good career change.

Stanton: I see.........I know you were at the club on Tuesday the fourth The waiters indicated that you didn't leave until eight...................Well thank you for your time. I may be back.

(He leaves)

Andrea: Why didn't you tell him what a misery that colonel was?

Dexter: We're in the military. You don't talk about your superiors,.......... not if want to stay out of trouble.

Andrea: You never thought that way before. You were tougher.

Dexter: We need to stay alive.........You can't survive with toughness......Three more years of this .... and we'll get our lives back.

Andrea: Thank God we're not in for twenty!

(the lights go out.)
(Stanton returns and now he's with the Gordons. Lights on)

Stanton: Good evening. I'm Colonel Walter Stanton with the JAG....................

Polly: We know ....Word gets around pretty fast on an air force base.

Stanton: I hope I'm not disturbing your dinner............

Polly: No ....We were planning to eat later at the club. How can we help you?

Stanton: Well I would appreciate any information you may have about Colonel Compagne's activities that might shed light on his ....problem.

Gordon: Not really.............He was pretty tough on everyone...............hard to get along with...............

Stanton: You may know his aide Captain Norris kept a log of his where-abouts. Routine for a hospital commander...............I guess................He was logged as being at your home several times................in the afternoons...................

Polly: That disgusting man...............He was making a move on me...........I threw him out........

Gordon: Polly told me about that. I had it out with him recently.................. He swore there was no evil intent.......... That bastard swore he would never come to my home again.

Polly: He didn't.

Stanton: I guess he was meeting some of his................ conquests....................... at a motel off base............Sorry to have to bring this up .... But we have to be thorough. ....Were there others...................?

Gordon: I won't comment on that. I'm sure you already have some people in mind. It doesn't involve Polly.

Stanton: I understand you completed your residency at UCLA and are paying back time to the air Force.

Polly: Yes ....and they're getting the best deal. Bob is a brilliant surgeon.........He should be in academic practice now.

Stanton: Well that's the Air Force deal.........if you'd rather not be conscripted. Particularly since resident salaries hover around seventy dollars a month. ..... and you were paid as a first lieutenant................ What kind of research were you carrying out in your dog lab?

Gordon: We were injecting various drugs into dogs on bypass and monitoring cardiac activity.

Stanton: Really interesting. Using any neurotoxins?...........

Gordon: Why yes. Some of the drugs are used routinely in Anesthesia you know. We were determining the effect of various doses on cardiac activity during surgery. Why are you asking about neurotoxins.

Stanton: Oh just curious. Some of these are derived from poisons used by ....inhabitants .... in the torrid zones. I believe they get it from frogs.

Gordon: That's true, I suppose. Many of our drugs are derived that way.

Stanton: Who else was involved?

Gordon: Doctor George Anderson was assisting me and we got Nurse Matz to give anesthesia and inject the drugs...............She's been very cooperative.

Stanton: Thanks. You work closely with lieutenants Matz and Smith in the OR also................

Polly: Don't start any stupid rumors..........My husband is very handsome and attracts interest. But he's been as loyal ....as have I.

Stanton: I'm sorry. I didn't mean to suggest any impropriety.

Polly: We've had Roberta over to our house many times. She's a close friend. I like Marni also…………

Stanton: I understand. ………. Did you enjoy your sojourn in Central Africa with special ops?

Gordon: I'm afraid I can't comment on that either.

Stanton: Yes……………Well I'll be leaving. I won't keep you from your dinner appointment. Are you meeting with the Dexters?

Polly: Yes.

Stanton: I know you had dinner with them on the fourth.. You arrived at about six.

Gordon: You've got all the details.

(He leaves)

Polly: That dog. He'll dig until he finds somebody to pin this on.

Gordon: You're right about that.

(Lights out. When they come on we're at the home of the Andersons)

Stanton: Good evening. I'm colonel Walter Stanton with JAG in Washington. I suppose you know all about my mission here.

Anderson: Yes, of course, It's all over the base.

Marge: Please sit down can I get you anything?………… Some scotch?……………

Stanton:	No thanks. I'll be at the officer's club later.....Have a drink there.
Marge:	We learned about drinking in the Air Force. Our first day here our neighbors dropped in to help us unpack ....They finished all the booze we had shipped here from Gunter. ...We have to restock every time someone visits. But it's so cheap at the PX.........
Anderson:	I'm sure Colonel Stanton is familiar with the Air Force culture.
Stanton:	Yes .... There's a lot of free time to contend with in the military ....I have a few questions that need some clarification. How well did you know Colonel Compagne? ....Get along with him?...............
Anderson:	I knew him only as Hospital Commander. We didn't talk much.
Stanton:	That's strange .... We logged him as visiting here once or twice.
Marge:	He may have stopped by to see if everything was ok.................. I believe he liked to check up on the doctor's homes. ....Said it made for better working conditions...........
Anderson:	I believe he did make rounds at some of the doctor's homes............ I didn't know he was here.
Stanton:	Have either of you ever been to the Sunset Motel near the base?
Anderson:	Never been there .....What is this about?......... Why these questions?.........
Marge:	No...........never...........

Stanton: Don't get upset. These are just routine...........I understand you worked with Doctor Gordon in the lab. What drugs were you injecting.

Anderson: Roberta did most of the injections. Mostly neurotoxins......You know the stuff they use for relaxation under anesthesia.......... We have a slew of data and are preparing a paper for the Armed Services Research Seminar in August. Expect to get it published.

Stanton: That's great for the Air Force. Was there a particular interest that nurse Matz had in these experiments? Was she just being helpful or was there another interest?

Anderson: Boy you've got a dirty mind! Roberta was a splendid assistant. She was always helpful and was glad to assist us in these experiments. She may have been attracted to Bob at one time .... but that developed into a good friendship with both Gordons. I think you ought to find another tree to bark up.

Stanton: Sorry.....Just trying to be complete. You two haven't been married very long...........

Marge: No we met during George's residency....... He's got four more years to go. I .was a singer with a band when we met................ I ....We didn't figure it would take so long before he went into practice..Now he's thinking of staying in for his twenty..........and then go out on a pension...................... Why did you bring up that motel?..............

Stanton: Compagne checked in there several times ....The clerk thought he remembered the lady................. but he's not certain................

Anderson: That can't have anything to do with us.

Stanton: I don't think it does................. Is there anything else you might want to say?

Anderson: No!.............You might want to talk to the Jamesons.

Stanton: I already have. .... Nice door to the kitchen, by the way, but it blocks the entrance.......You ought to have it taken down............ Thanks for your help. Goodbye for now. We'll meet in a few days with some of the others.

(He exits)

Anderson: *(turns toward his wife)* I THINK WE'D BETTER HAVE A TALK!

(Lights out)

ACT III
Scene 2

(We are back in col. Compagne's office. All the principles are seated stage right. They include the Jamesons, the Andersons, the Gordons, Dexters and the neurologists Horn and Dorrin captains Norris and Fitzhugh and nurses Smith and Matz. Colonel Stanton is in front of the desk and addressing the group.)

Stanton: Thank you all for gathering here tonight so promptly. I'm certain you will be interested in my findings. I will say first off that after concluding my investigation I can be certain that I know what happened to the Colonel.

Let us review what is known: Campagne was a somewhat ruthless leader. He made enemies in many of his Air Force assignments. He was also known as a lady's man. .... having affairs with several women. Norris had him signed out to a certain nearby motel on occasions when he was................entertaining his guests.

Jameson: But that's a poor reason for murder. He wasn't apt to tell anyone about that. And certainly it was consensual. Unless ....

Stanton: Yes... Unless a husband found out about it. But it seemed to me that a gun might be a more appropriate method of retaliation in that circumstance. The availability of arms on base would make that the logical choice. .... But the colonel was poisoned.

Anderson: I still think that a man could do it.

34

Stanton: Let us continue.

Colonel Compagne was alone in his office when the pizza was delivered. Captain Norris found it on his desk when he returned from his rounds. Before signing out he brought the box to the colonel who had, as usual, planned to work a little late. The pizza order was a normal Tuesday night habit and most everyone was aware of it. That was at six o'clock.

The box was unusual in that it had been stapled shut, necessitating some effort in opening it. He pricked his finger with the effort The reaction must have been almost instantaneous indicating that the poison was rapidly active. I'm basing that on the fact that the base MPs received a call at six ten and were here in ten minutes.

I would guess it was similar to Batrachotoxin, a deadly poison found in the skin of frogs and used by natives in the jungle to arm deadly darts used in hunting.

Gordon: But that's one of the drugs we were using
....

Stanton: Yes I know! However the knowledge of this drug would be available to anyone living in the tropics...............or central Africa or.........working in the OR.

For the average killer, however, cyanide would be a logical choice. Easily available fast, tasteless, and deadly in small amounts. None was found in our toxicology studies. But this neurotoxin was found over the pepperoni.

But why the staples and who made the call to the MPs. This puzzled me for a while ....
Then I remembered .....these neurotoxins are not toxic if ingested. They would change the taste of the pizza.......... However in order to be effective they need to be given by injection. ....Since the pepperoni was laced with it the perpetrator did not know that it would not work or................. knew that it wouldn't be effective............. But again the

staples .... only a minuscule amount could be delivered.............maybe enough to kill a monkey .... but not an Air Force Colonel...................

Gordon: So this was not attempt to kill.................

Stanton: Exactly!..............

(At this moment Colonel Compagne enters and strides to Center Stage)

Fitzhugh: You mean that rat is still alive???

Stanton: And of course it didn't. There is still the possibility that it was a warning attempt that went awry. .... but the call was made to preclude that.

Compagne: There's going to be hell to pay when I get back to that desk.

Stanton: I need to conclude .... The staples were used to cover up the fact that the box had been torn when the poison was added. It then occurred to the caller that serious injury could take place........ and thus the early call. The whole affair was meant to frighten the Colonel not kill him.

Gordon: I brought that poison home from Africa for these experiments. But I didn't poison .... Many people could have had access..............

Stanton: Yes, I know..........The call to the MPs   after analysis..........was made by the disguised voice of a ....woman. Only our nurse anesthetist would be familiar with this drug.............isn't that true ....Lieutenant Matz.

Compagne: Roberta.............why

Matz: As a warning to stay away from Polly. You won't

get a chance to ruin the Gordons like you have with other families.

Stanton: No you didn't do it. Not alone....You would have known that this toxin has no effect if administered orally. It would only affect the taste of the food. No need to panic. But someone you worked alongside may not have known how lethal it might be on an injured finger. Only one person fits this description........When she told you about the staples, you did panic and made the call to the base police......... Maybe Nurse Smith would like to say something.

Smith: I'm not saying anything, except that Colonel Compagne needs to be reeled in. He's used his authority to badger women to accept his advances for too long............................

Compagne: I want all the details. I'll have General Johnson convene a court martial...........

Stanton: I don't think so...... Washington does not relish having the Air Force dragged through the dailies. You suffered the equivalent of a good sock on the head............................... I contacted your friend Battaglia and guess what..........you're joining Fitzhugh in the Azores next week.

Fitzhugh: Oh ...great!

Stanton: As for you nurse Matz............... Get that paper published and we'll see what we can do. .... but for Nurse Smith............... there will be a further investigation.........
We may have some bad things to say about Air Force medicine....................
But we won't question the value of Air Force justice.

THE END (CURTAIN LIGHTS OUT)

DANSE MACABRE

AN ORIGINAL PLAY

BY

BERNARD GARDNER

THE PLAYERS
(In order of appearance)

Man #1 and Man #2

Sir James Ellis Hartwick Lord of the manor and wealthiest member of the
community

Anthony Caleb McGuire Developer and builder

Arthur Towers.

Man#3 and Man#4

Colleague

Professor Hugh Dudley Professor of English Literature at Boyden College

Man#5, Surgeon #1 and Surgeon #2 and Man at the Table

Dr. George Sullivan Surgeon at the Hartwick Clinic

Hiram Hartstone Director of the Bank

His Assistant at the Bank

Elena Brams.

Henrietta Towers

Lorraine Watts-Jones

Woman Friend of Doctor Sullivan.

Maryanne

Abigail Hartstone.

John Watts Butler to the Hartwick Estate

Constable Henry Barcroft Local law enforcement officer

DANSE MACABRE
PROLOGUE:

This play is concerned with the inevitable lust for power that exists in the minds of those of great wealth. It is set in England in the 1950s but the exact location is immaterial. Sir James Hartwick controls his shire due to his generous use of vast amounts of money. He believes that he can influence the behavior of the key citizens and develop a master plan for his community. But can anyone fit people into preconceived molds? Can power generate sufficient force to influence human behavior? We know that the dictator exists by dint of fear but is it a permanent state? On what levels does human behavior return to its basic motivations and reject the force attempting to mold it? A second strong element is the accuracy with which the mold is chosen. Does the wielder of power fit the individual into a chosen mold or will that person resist the attempt by dint of the fact that he really doesn't fit or doesn't want to fit, and thus return to his basic nature?

ACT I
SCENE 1

As the curtain rises center stage is set with a boardroom table transversely. Sir James is facing the audience on the far side. Seated with backs to the audience are five men in dark suits. Sir James is spotted and wearing a dark 3 piece suit. The central action is in a ghostly light. There is space at either side for the alternative action which shifts from the main scene. Each man is just a segment of Sir James' mind as he controls both the questions and responses.

Man #1: How certain are we that our plan will work?

Man #2.: Yes. The problem on Queensway may have set things back.

Sir James: The remedy is already activated. Remember the plan requires time. Time is always the key. It opens the door to the future.

Man #1: Can we trust the players? Will they perform as predicted?

Sir James: Human behavior is often perfidious. But with provision of sufficient opportunity and motivation it can be controlled and directed.

Man # 1: I hope you are correct.

Sir James: Yes!. We will see.

Lights off.

Stage right is set up as an office. A desk and a small lamp (plus spots) provide light. In a large chair behind the desk sits Anthony. In front in a comfortable chair sits Arthur.

Anthony: Arthur... so good to see you. It's been a while.

Arthur: Quite right!,,,,,,,,,,,, You have a beautiful office............ My sister loves it here.

Anthony: She's extremely competent. Very dedicated. ..... But it's an honor to have you visit. Can I help you with something .... anything? Just let me know. Perhaps some sherry..............

Arthur: No not personally, but your good sherry........... yes I'll try a bit of that. ..*(Anthony pours two small sherries Arthur sips some)* Excellent. .... I just wanted to talk a bit. By the way ..... sorry about that Queensway business............ What could possibly have caused such a mess?

Anthony: Any number of things. ...Mostly, I suppose the blueprints ....the plan must have been faulty.

Arthur rises and takes a few steps. Then he leans across the desk towards Anthony.

Arthur: Oh I'm sure that's the problem.

Arthur takes a few steps toward the corner of the desk.

Arthur: You know ....there'll have to be an investigation....

Anthony rises and takes a few steps toward the opposite corner of the desk.

Anthony: It's inevitable. There's bound to be bad publicity. We've been doing pretty well up to now. Thank God no one was injured.

Arthur: I know ....Henrietta keeps me up to date.

Anthony: Sure!....And how is it going with you? I hear that a
                 run for parliament is a possibility.

Arthur: Oh.. Is that common talk now? Well anything is
                 possible.

Anthony: Yes... an investigation.......... I don't suppose.........
                 there's something.......... I mean....nothing
                 dishonest.

*They circle the desk slowly.   Arthur moves gradually toward Anthony's
chair.*

Arthur: I never met a situation where something couldn't
                 be done..........Nothing dishonest....How's
                 Henrietta doing? I mean I know she's a terrific
                 secretary and all that...........

Anthony gradually moves toward Arthur's chair.

Anthony: Who do you think will run the show?...

Arthur sits in Anthony's chair.

Arthur: Why this is really comfortable!.............I
                 understand the committee will probably fall into
                 my bailiwick

Anthony sits in Arthur's chair.

Anthony: Really!!.....That would be a fortunate break. That
                 architect may have had some previous problems.

Arthur: Oh I'm certain there'll be something turned
                 up............... Don't you think Henrietta is a pretty
                 lady............

Lights off.

Lights on the board table.

Man# 3:	You know Chadwick should be retiring soon. The college will need to recruit a new president in a few years.
Sir James:	Chadwick will be no great loss. He hasn't produced a significant piece of literature in two decades. He's holding the college back.
Man#4:	We'll probably need a search committee made up of local board members.
Sir James:	That's a laugh! ....We'll be lucky if the local board members can find the board room at the college.
Man # 4:	Yes....... I don't think they have ever had a meeting. They will probably go outside borough to recruit.
Sir James:	Never a good move! New blood breeds new ideas and new ideas breed conflict. The last thing we need is student opinion getting involved in the search.
Man #3:	But who would be a good inside candidate?.......... You're surely not conti plating putting Dudley up?
Sir James:	His new novel received kudos from the Times.
Man#4:	.................But the rumors..............
Sir James:	Behavior can be modified! Remember opportunity and motivation. .... He'll be elected Dean next year....
Man #4:	I certainly hope he can be controlled.

Sir James:	Anyone can be controlled.
Man #4:	What about the older professors. They will all consider themselves candidates.
Sir James:	I will arrange for the main ones to be on sabbatical when Chadwick announces and the committee is formed.

Lights off.

Stage right is now set up as a library office - desk, computer etc. comfortable chairs , bookshelves, etc. High and a colleague are seated and conversing. Hugh smoking his pipe.

Colleague:	What a sensational review. You are clearly the darling of the critics.
Hugh:	Hardly. It was a stroke of luck that Harrington got the call. He and I were on a panel together last Spring. I had an opportunity to support his views on the literary awards.
Colleague:	I'll say!.... Did you have much editorial control?
Hugh:	God no!! I had to fight through three editorial reviews before it was finally accepted. June Ross was assigned to me and her suggestions were generally very sound.
Colleague:	I suppose you'll be moving now.
Hugh:	Not at all. My benefactors here have apparently offered to support me for Dean. It will certainly be a relief from having to spend so much time teaching classes.
Colleague:	I thought you loved to work with students....Are the rumors.............................

Hugh: Don't be foolish.........Rumors are rarely true - otherwise they become accusations!

Colleague: Will the department support your promotion.

Hugh: Of course! It opens a job at the top.........for. which each member is convinced he deserves consideration.

Colleague: Hugh you need a good woman to settle down .

Hugh: Well there is a profusion of available women. A good woman .... that may require more thought............... and probably some good fortune..........

Colleague: It will certainly improve your stature at the college.

Hugh: Yes!........perhaps my guardian angel will strike upon someone.....appropriate.

Lights out.

Lights on the boardroom table.

Man #5: The College alone will not provide notoriety for our borough.

Sir James: Of course!   You are correct. I believe we need something in an advanced field.,,,,,, Building a library at the college will help but by itself will not do the job.

Man#5: What do you have in mind?

Sir James: Research...Medical research...At present the clinic is mediocre. We will build a research wing and recruit personnel.

Man #5:	We will need a dynamic leader. Do you have someone in mind?
Sir James:	Yes.- George Sullivan. He meets the criteria. Although he is a mediocre surgeon he has published extensively and is well known in the academic community.
Man #5:	Mostly for carousing! I suppose that's a positive. Everyone seems to enjoy his company.
Sir James:	We will find a way of curtailing his ....extra curricular activities.
Man #5:	He makes plenty of money. How will you motivate him?
Sir James:	Money?....Money? That's not a prime motivator! There are two major motivators: FEAR and POWER. Fear of loss of position, or personal harm and the lust for power to control destiny. Sullivan will yield to his desire to lead the institution!

Lights switch to stage left. Scene is set up as an OR lounge for surgeons and OR personnel. A sofa is present with two men in scrubs are seated. Another man is seated at a small table with three chairs having a bag lunch. Sullivan walks in and one of the couch sitters rises and bows.

Surgeon #1:	My hero! Your paper in the Annals is excellent. Good piece of research.
Surgeon#2:	How do you find the time?
George:	The answer is .... good assistants and a research fellow! It's a winning combination.
Surgeon#2:	Still needs the ideas and supervision.
George:	Thanks guys.

Man at Table:	Are you going to Nancy's party?
George:	Wouldn't mis it.
Surgeon#1:	How do you manage such an active social life?
George:	The answer is ....good assistants and a research fellow! Look you know my philosophy: Spend 30 years smoking to develop collaterals and the next 30 years drinking to keep them open. I am in the latter stages.
Surgeon #2:	That's a great operation Norris developed. He's doing another one today.
George:	You're right Better for him to stay in the OR. Get rid of the administrative burden
Surgeon#2:	I guess you can handle that end. Leave time for more parties.

George lifts his coffee cup as in a toast. Lights out .

Back on the board table.

Man#1:	We're going to need some heavy funding.
Sir James:	I don't expect a problem.
Man#2:	Should we purchase a bank to cover the mortgages?
Sir James:	Not necessary. We'll use Abigail's bank. She'll see to the financing.
Man#2:	I suppose.......... if we can keep Hiram out of the picture. He certainly isn't very knowledgeable about the banking business.

Sir James:	We'll see about getting him some help.

Lights off and shift to stage left where we find Hiram sitting behind his desk and a bank assistant standing in front of the desk.

Hiram:	Why was the supermarket loan turned down?
Assistant:	I'm sorry sir. The loan committee felt that the security was insufficient. The opening of the new discount food court would have considerably cut into their future operations.
Hiram:	The loan committee? Why wasn't I advised of the meeting. I should have attended.

I wasn't informed about the risks.

Assistant:	I'm very sorry. But your wife was present. I assumed you were fully informed.
Hiram:	Assumed?,,.............. Assumed? I don't count on you to assume! You should reevaluate your allegiances.
Assistant:	Yes, of course.
Hiram:	My wife.......... my wife.................

Lights off back again on the board table.

Sir James:	I believe we have covered all of the agenda. Shall we adjourn?
Man#4:	I agree. May I ask you one question?
Sir James:	Yes?
Man #4:	You are expending an enormous effort on these projects. Surely the borough will prosper. While

this will enhance your notoriety you already have amassed a great fortune. Why do you need to extend yourself further?

Sir James: My friend ....Don't you understand?   THIS IS MY MOUNTAIN...............THIS IS MY K-2!

Curtain end of scene 1.

ACT I
SCENE 2

(As the curtain rises the stage is set as a dance floor. Above is a crystal ball that rotates later in the act. In the background is a Punch and Judy stage on which several puppets sit. To the right stage background is the storefront window of a dollmaker's shop, reminiscent of "Copellia".

Sir James Hartwick enters from stage left. He is in tails and is carrying a music stand. He places it down stage left facing the stage and takes out a baton. He taps the stand several times and begins to conduct an imaginary orchestra. As he begins the music starts and the song "Say it isn't so" is played.)

(The first couple on the dance floor are Anthony and Elena. As they slowly turn we can hear the conversation. Each couple enter from upstage right, diagonally across from Sir James. At the upper stage left is a desk with accouterments and a typewriter. It is in darkness.)

Elena:	But I thought we were going to set the date tonight...
Anthony:	Impossible! I may have some trouble brewing...... I can't commit until this problem is solved.
Elena:	I never thought you really wanted to commit............It's not in your character.
Anthony:	Please bear with me on this. We'll have another look at us when this is all settled.
Elena:	Well don't look at us in a mirror......... I may not be at your side.
Anthony:	Elena ... please............It may only be a few months.

Elena: A few months or a few years...It's been too long already. There's always going to be something ....some shadow standing between us. I'm not sure I can commit any more either.

Anthony: I beg you......be patient a while.............. The time will come ....

Elena: Maybe!................or it may never come.

(They dance slowly off the floor and exit stage right. The desk at the upper left is now spotted. Henrietta is busy typing as her brother enters and gives her a quick buss on the cheek.)

Arthur: Hi sis..........How's things in the building business? Writing up a few new contracts?

Henrietta: Hi Arty. Why so chipper? You know we haven't had any new contracts since the building collapsed.

Arthur: And you're not likely to get one until the investigation is over. You know I'm heading it up.

Henrietta: I've heard.............. Appointed by the bigwigs weren't you? Is Anthony...Mr. McGuire I mean .....Going to be in trouble.?

Anthony: I can't discuss any of that business.,,,,,,,,,,, This may be a golden opportunity ...for you..you know.

Henrietta: What on earth are you talking about? Don't start one of your plots. I'm just his   secretary.

Anthony: Yes his mooning secretary............I've seen that look in your eyes when he's around.
Look at you .....you're blushing now.
(Henrietta takes a small mirror from her purse, glances at it and sighs.)
I'm meeting with him again today. Just do

your secretarial duties and leave plans and plots to me...........and the fates.*(He raises his arm and points toward Sir James. The lights go black.)*

(The second couple dance into view as the music plays louder. It is Hugh and Lorraine dancing a slow foxtrot to "Stardust" played without vocal. The music dims as they converse.)

Hugh: You look especially lovely tonight. Are you studying hard?

Lorraine: Why thank you ..kind professor! I must be ..... I've received excellent grades. In fact good enough to guarantee admission for my masters in business administration.

Hugh: I assume you'll be leaving us for a while. ..... Why not stay here and study in the English Department? ....I find you a particularly.......adept...student.

Lorraine: Being an academician was never in my plans. ..... I'm sorry ....I didn't intend to step on your feelings.

Hugh: Oh.....I know.......... I never really pictured you in an academic lifestyle..... Will you ever return?

Lorraine: Possibly...It's my home..but not at the college. I think a farewell kiss might be appropriate. *(They kiss briefly.)* Good night sweet prince... *(she turns slowly. They separate as she slowly walks toward the exit. Hugh utters his final line.)*

Hugh: Fear not. My noble heart will not be crackt. *(At this moment Elena appears behind Hugh. He turns slowly and sees her. They eye each other and as the music gets louder they both exit close to one another but not together.)*

(A new song begins. It is " Ain't we got fun" vocal. George Sullivan and a woman are dancing. As they circle George is waving a cocktail glass and taking sips.)

George: Party, party, party. Ain't we got fun?

Woman: I love it. Particularly after midnight..............

(As they continue the dance Maryanne appears on stage. She watches for a while then slowly approaches the couple and cuts in. She grabs the arm of the woman and turns her toward the exit. The woman leaves the stage. She then takes the glass away from George. The music slows to "I get a kick out of you" They dance a and leave stage left.)

(The music now changes to "I'm losing my mind" (Sondheim). Hiram and Abigail are dancing. They are clearly arguing as the music dims.)

Hiram: But I don't seem to have any responsibility at the bank.

Abigail: But of course you do..............You're the managing director. ....You sign everything.

Hiram: My signature isn't worth a twit. If there is a major decision to be made it's punted up to   you.

Abigail: Well the old timers still have respect for my father. That's why he left it to me. He felt that restressing the family involvement would reassure our customers and depositors.

Hiram: That's nonsense! .... If I'm part of this family I need to have some control.....Why haven't you given me a share of the stock?

Abigail: George we've been over this time and again. My plan is to have Jimmie take over..... it's my father's wish. I am just a guardian of his inheritance. Let's not argue............

Hiram: That's the way we always end it. LET'S NOT ARGUE. Well let's argue! I think you're wrong and I should be a part owner...... that is ..I assume that I'm Jimmie's father...

Abigail: THAT'S DISGUSTING!...   I won't allow this to continue...........

(Abigail turns rapidly and storms off the stage exit left. George turns toward that side and looks after her. After a few beats we hear a car crash offstage. A moment later Hiram turns and drops his head in his hands burying his face. Slowly from stage right Lorraine appears. She moves center stage and appears lost. She looks up and slowly turns and sees Hiram. She walks slowly toward him. He raises his head and looks at her. As the music rises and plays They both walk offstage left . Lights dim. The dance light above begins to circle as the dance floor theme. Sir James begins to conduct The song is "Change Partners" sung by Fred Astaire and the couples appear on stage dancing. First are Hugh and Elena then in rapid order Anthony and Henrietta, George and Maryanne and Hiram and Lorraine. As they dance the music gets louder and the lights go off. End of act I.)

ACT II
SCENE 1

(Five Years Later. ......Music is playing "As Time Goes By". It fades as the scene starts)

SETTING: The stage is dark. Previously placed props are not visible. The actors are in position at the four corners of the stage. As each pair are speaking they will be highlighted by a single spotlight.   The actors face offstage and turn and move toward center stage as their parts come up.

The first pair are Professor Hugh Dudley and his wife Elena.
   The doorbell rings. Spot comes on to visualize Elena who appears to collect a letter at the door.   She and Hugh are placed upstage right.

Elena: Hugh,,, *She turns* Hugh... Some man just delivered a letter.

Hugh: Special delivery? *He enters the area of the spotlight.* What's that all about? There's a mail delivery today!

Elena: I know. But it wasn't the post. It's addressed to both of us. *She holds it up to the light.*

Hugh: Oh for God's sake .... Open it up.

Elena tears the envelope open and removes an invitation. She reads it and starts to hand it to Hugh. Hugh grabs at it.

Hugh: What's this...... an invitation?

Elena: What a clever observation.

Hugh: Oh don't be so smug. .... It's from Hartwick. He requests that we come to the manor on Saturday evening for after dinner drinks and "conversation". What the hell does he want to converse about? .... and I like his use of ...."request".

Elena: Maybe it has something to do with your election to College President? There isn't any trouble is there?

Hugh: Not likely. Besides the board will bow, as usual, to the desire of the students. As long as the faculty doesn't suspect I'll do away with tenure in a year they won't interfere.

Elena: Well you certainly won't get any trouble from the students.................especially the ladies!

Hugh: Now don't start that again. That was over a long time ago..................... Besides she's got enough to handle with the bank .... and her boss.

Elena: Well you never should ....

Hugh: WILL YOU PLEASE STOP. If it weren't for your infernal nagging............

Elena: Sure I'm to blame!.... I probably am .... I should have sewn your zipper closed.

Hugh: Oh Please................

Elena: The Manor? I don't think anyone I know has seen the insides of that place. It's huge.

Hugh: I believe he has his collections there. He's quite a collector of antiques and paintings ....and his library has a first edition of Milton's Paradise Lost....I'd love to see that.

Elena: I hardly think he's inviting us for a tour.

Hugh: Yes, of course.............. I wonder who else will be invited. We'd better respond. We'll go

Elena: Well since he's contributing a new Library to the College I'd say we'd better go.

Hugh: Why the conversation? This is very mysterious .... and I HATE MYSTERIES!

Spot goes off

After 15 seconds spot goes on at lower right stage where it picks up Maryanne in a nurse's uniform George is nearby, and comes into view on his cue.

Maryanne: George, ... Doctor Sullivan...... A fellow just dropped this off at the admissions desk. It looks like an invitation .... Addressed to you.

George: An invitation. What on earth for ... probably another one of those damn pharmaceutical dinners. I don't think I can stand another antibiotic sales pitch.

Maryanne hands him the envelope which he tears open.

George: Well I'll be ...... It's from Sir James ...... An invitation to after dinner drinks and conversation. What can that be about?

Maryanne: Let me see. For Saturday 10 PM. I have no idea. ..... Why mention drinks? .....You don't think.....

George: Now don't start that again! Since he's funding a good part of our research building I'd better be

62

prepared to go. Ten PM what an ungodly hour for a party.

Maryanne: Just try and control yourself. We don't know who else will be there.

George: Now stop!...... I don't drink before Surgery. I AM in complete control.

Maryanne: Sure!....... Two days ago you started mixing Martinis in the Intensive Care Unit.

George: Well it woke up those two retired golfers in beds 3 and 4.

Maryanne: Yeah..............The nurses started recording blood pressures on the patients' nightgowns.

George: Well it was a going away party for Janet.

Maryanne: Going away? .... She's being committed to the psych ward.

George: Well a party's a party. Besides I no longer have a nightcap before surgery.

Maryanne: Your nightcaps have a strange tendency to run into breakfast. .... It's not surgery. It's the emergency call you should give up.

George: Please stop! I am in complete control .... I will not shame myself and risk the Research Building...... or my position here for that matter. I suppose that Abigail will be there.

Maryanne: She probably still blames you for
....

George: So what if she does................. A problem in the ER................... It happens all the time.

Maryanne: There's no need to advertise your ,,,,,,,,propensities............Never-the-less I am coming with you. ...I can converse also .... and you may need my protection.

George: If you insist.... I'll be in my office. PLEASE SEE THAT I'M NOT DISTURBED.

Spotlight off 15 seconds

Spotlight picks up upstage left where Lorraine is sitting at a small desk writing... using her left hand. She looks up and slowly fingers the invitation envelope. She opens it carefully using a letter opener with he left hand. Hiram Hartstone enters into the light.

Lorraine: It's from Sir James. *She looks at the letter for a beat, turns and hands it to Hiram.*

Hiram: An invitation to after dinner drinks and conversation ... Saturday night. I dearsay I'd better pay attention to this. Is it a private audience or a party .... can't make it out. Be bad protocol to see who else was invited.

Lorraine: Well you certainly can't do that without possibly riling up a few bad feelings for someone who wasn't invited.

Hiram: Of course...course. Could it be bank business?......... He is our largest depositor.
　　Well you'd better send off an affirmative response.

Lorraine: What about Abigail? You know he'll expect her to be there. The letter is addressed to you both.

Hiram: Yes...yes ...She still owns the bank..... But she'll never go. She hasn't been out since the accident. She still blames Sullivan for Jimmie's loss ... and her scars. She'll never appear publically again ... or so she says.

Lorraine: She'll have to go. This could be important to the bank. You'll have to talk her into it. It's could be an important conversation. Hiram you know we are overextended on the borrowing. If anything happened to these projects ....

Hiram: Yes...yes I suppose you're right on target. I'll propose it to her tonight...give her a few days to mull it over. It would be too embarrassing not to have her present. We've got a lot to consider. ...Yes we are heavily mortgaged. Thank God you are running things so well. You know if it weren't .... *(he touches her shoulder)....* well I owe you some thanks for handling the mortgages on the new buildings...............

Lorraine: It's been a pleasure working here............... and being with you. We've both learned alot ....about the banking business.

Hiram: Yes. Abigail will be thankful for the profits this year.

Lorraine: I'm sure she will be there when she's made to realize the importance to the bank. IN FACT I'M ABSOLUTELY CERTAIN SHE'LL BE THERE ON SATURDAY!

Lorraine stands... turns to Hiram   They embrace   Spotlight off for 15 seconds

Spotlight on downstage left. It picks up Anthony McGuire and his wife Henrietta. He is sitting, she is standing alongside holding the invitation envelope. She is wearing a fur jacket and ostentatious jewelry.

Henrietta: What an absurd way of delivering an invitation!

Anthony:	As long as it's not from the authorities. Who sent it ... and for what? Not one of those infernal charity affairs I trust.
Henrietta:	No. It's from Sir James. He wants us to come to his home for "after dinner drinks and conversation".
Anthony:	What? Both of us?
Henrietta:	Yes. It's addressed to Mr. And Mrs. It's for Saturday night 10 PM. We'll have to cancel our dinner party. It's our fifth anniversary..................I don't suppose he would do this another night.
Anthony:	Don't be ridiculous. One doesn't ask Sir James to alter his schedule. We just acquiesce What is this conversation thing? What does he want to talk about?
Henrietta:	It couldn't possibly be related ... to that building......
Anthony:	*(interrupting)* Now stop! That was five years ago..... It was thoroughly investigated.
Henrietta:	By my brother.
Anthony:	We ALL did very nicely on that one. ....If that were a problem he wouldn't have given me the library and research center to build. We stand to clear a bundle on this.
Henrietta:	You're not up to that old ploy again, are you? Please let's not compromise everything we have.
Anthony:	No...No...no shenanigans this time. I'm fully covered.............

Henrietta: Nevertheless I'm concerned. This is all very strange... very irregular.

Anthony: I wouldn't worry... in fact I'M NOT IN THE LEAST WORRIED.

Spot off

ACT II
SCENE 2

Music introduction is "Stormy Weather" sung by Lena Horne

The stage is fully lit. The setting includes a large serving piece set up as a bar. Several bottles of whiskey at the rear. A large bucket of ice to the right. Glasses are present in a large silver tray. They are brandy snifters and sherry (port) glasses. Two large carafes are present one to the right of the glasses contains Brandy (apple juice) the other to the left of the glasses contains vintage port (grape juice).

The stage is bounded by furniture consisting of a large sofa to the right margin, and two large soft chairs to the left margin. Two imaginary exits are present to the upstage left and right. Enough comfortable seating is present for nine people. Assorted small tables and lamps to indicate a comfortable room with enough center stage for the action.

It is storming outside. Claps of thunder can be heard. Music
....

Six guests have already arrived and are milling about in the room, conversing and drinking either port or brandy. John Watts is serving the drinks. George approaches the bar and receives a brandy and watches as John takes some for himself. This is repeated as a drink is served to Anthony. George is delighted at the antics of John. Abigail Hartstone wearing a dark puffy suit is in a wheel chair quietly sitting be herself. She has a dark hat with a heavy veil which covers her face. At the upper right corner, outside the room a doorbell sounds as the last guests arrive (professor and Mrs Dudley). They are soaked and hand their umbrella and topcoats to the butler who then escorts them into the room. Others nod in recognition some offer to shake hands.

The din of conversation gradually diminishes as a clap of thunder is heard. The guests gravitate to their seats.

As the evening progresses John Watts continues to serve drinks to the guests from the bar set up. Each drink he hands to a guest (a few refuse) he takes a quiet swallow for himself. He grows slowly more tipsy. This is an aside and should not interfere with the action.

Professor Dudley: What a blasted night. I guess we're all here for conversation.

Hiram Hartstone: Say something amusing Hugh... you know something clever from one of your courses.

Anthony McGuire: Don't be a boor Hiram. Leave him alone. None of us seems to know what's going on.

George Sullivan: Well the brandy is excellent. Let's enjoy. Cheers! (*He takes a sip after holding the snifter high.*)

Elena: You should be a connoisseur by now.

Anthony: You're in rather a bad mood tonight.

Henrietta: Yes WE'VE had to cancel a dinner ...for this. (*John walks to Henrietta and hands her a snifter of brandy. She holds it in the air...*) I do hope this is that famous Louis the twelfth.

John: I believe you mean Louis the thirteenth ma'am.

(At this time Elena Dudley slowly saunters over to Henrietta and peers at her dress and fur coat. With a pause she looks up and says..)

Elena: Daaahling...... You look ....so..................... WARM.

(Henrietta stares and flips her hand in the air)

George: Cancelled a party?..........Sorry about that. I guess we weren't invited.,,,,,,,,,,,,,,,,,, Saving money on booze?

Maryanne: George stay under control. That wasn't a nice thing to say.

George: You're right! How about something lighthearted.........Have you heard...... We have a new doctor on staff............... if you can't afford the operation....he touches up the xrays.

(The guests laugh)

A clap of thunder is heard. John walks slowly toward the door upstage right. Everyone is suddenly silent. A clock tolls eleven. At that moment Sir James Hartwick enters the room. All rise. He is accompanied by constable Barcroft. Sir James waves everyone to be seated

John Watts, the butler, approaches Abigail Hartstone in her wheelchair.

John Watts: May I get you some brandy ma'am.

Abigail: *she nods*

John pours some brandy in a snifter and hands it to her. She takes it with her left hand. He turns to Sir James.

John Watts: May I get you something from the bar sir?

Sir James: Not now John. Are you all comfortable? You have obviously guessed that there is a reason that I have asked you to be here tonight. ....

    I have had serious but pleasant business and social relations with all of you. Hugh, you have been Dean of Boyden College and I have agreed to build a new library for the school. It has been my pleasure to work with you these years and to follow your academic progress.

    George you have been director of the Hartwick clinic and have done a good job as Surgeon in chief. Your request to build a new research wing has met with the approval of my board and will soon be going forward. It would be a great honor to see progress in research in our borough.

Tony you have built several of our projects and will be responsible for directing the development of these new buildings here. We expect nothing but the finest and most modern facilities.

Hiram you have handled all of the financial details smoothly and we rely on your good judgement in raising the proper funds to support all of these efforts. And special thanks to your bank (*he turns and nods to Abigail*) for its efficient handling of these endeavors.

WE HAVE HOWEVER DISCOVERED A MAJOR PROBLEM WITH ONE OF YOU THAT MAY COMPROMISE ONE OR MORE PARTS OF OUR MASTER PLAN. THIS HAS RECENTLY COME TO MY ATTENTION .

I have asked Constable Barcroft to be present tonight. We are going to remedy this situation before it becomes public knowledge if that is at all possible. One of you knows what that problem is. I will allow that person one hour to consider all of the consequences. If by that time I am contacted and a full confession is obtained that individual will avoid the shame to be foisted on our community and will be escorted from the borough. I will not inform the constable of the deeds and that person is likely to avoid prosecution. However, if I am not contacted within the allotted time I will press the appropriate charges and Constable Barcroft will take whatever action is necessary.

For the rest of you.... This house is a treasure trove of collections. The library has several first editions which you may wish to inspect. There is a rare collection of miniature french sculpture in the billiard room. If you are interested in French renaissance painting there are several examples in the main upper corridors. The cellar has a world renowned collection of old port and several casks may be tasted.. Please feel free to enter any of the large rooms to see some of our Regency and Victorian furniture. John will guide you to the various areas of the manor. For that certain person .... I WILL BE IN MY STUDY. I IMPLORE YOU TO COME AND CLEAR THE AIR.

Accompanied by a clap of thunder Sir James turns and leaves the room. The others start to murmur to their partners. We can hear some of the conversations:

Hugh: Can this be possible? What on earth is happening.

Elena: He can't know! Lorraine would never have said anything. She's got other interests now.

Hugh: Still.... a professor and a student ..... I thought it was over............

Elena: Be quiet. This can't concern you. Be quiet. Nothing will happen.

Anthony: I thought that was all cleared up five years ago. The investigation ....there was no fault found.......... the architect took the blame.............. Your brother......

Henrietta: Could he possibly know about the committee? But that's all old hat! ....
     No. It must be something more recent....... one of the others...

Anthony: Yes ..... more recent..............

Hiram: He can't have looked into the financing. He's always left that to me. This is pure nonsense. It must be one of the others. Still this could ruin our bank..........

Abigail: *(In a hoarse voice)* Be still. It's not you!

George: What's this all about? Jail?   For what?

Maryanne: I told you to curb your drinking..... at least in public.. Look at that smug Abigail sitting there. ....She's never forgiven you.

George: That can't be it. That was years ago. I can't be blamed for an emergency........

Maryanne: You should never have taken emergency call ....

George: For God's sake be quiet.................

Maryanne: Yes .... I'll be quiet.

As the storm rages on the lights flicker but stay on. Slowly each of the guests leave the stage.

Couples breaking up in separate directions. John and constable Barcroft also leave. This includes Abigail who moves her own wheelchair out of the room. After a short delay a clap of thunder is heard and the lights go out. With the stage darkened and empty two shots ring out.

In a few seconds the lights go back on. The guests and John filter excitedly back into the room.

Loud murmurings are audible. "What happened?"   "Was that a shot?" "What was that noise?" All are back in the room except for Abigail, Barcroft and Sir James.

Hiram: Where's Abigail? What's happened? ....What's going on?

Barcroft: *(Entering the room excitedly - gun drawn.)* I have terrible news. *(He walks slowly around the room.)*........THERE'S BEEN A MURDER ....*(As he slowly circles people are aghast some begin sobbing softly others appear agitated. One cries out "who?" At the exact moment he reaches Hiram Hartstone, Sir James rushes into the room.)*

Mr Hartstone ... I'm sorry to tell you .....
YOUR WIFE HAS BEEN MURDERED.

LIGHTS OFF   END OF ACT TWO

ACT III

(The act is introduced by the music "Who" instrumental Tommy Dorsey. As the music fades lights on)

The act begins at the moment that the previous act ended. The players are in the same positions. As Barcroft deduces who the killer must be, he circles facing each suspect in turn. John Watts is stunned and carefully observes the suspects, and approaches each slowly as Barcroft addresses him.

Constable Barcroft: Mr. Hartstone..... I'm sorry to tell you ....YOUR WIFE HAS BEEN MURDERED!.................but as you know that wasn't your wife in that wheelchair...............IT WAS YOUR ASSISTANT LORRAINE. (*Gasps and confusion from the others. John Watts puts his head in his hands.*)
    You knew that! .... as did others in this room. Your wife is right handed but when she reached for her brandy she used her left hand. She gave herself away. Lorraine was known to be left-handed. But you had no motive to kill Lorraine. You were having an affair with her. You never told your wife about the invitation for fear that something might slip.

(He moves toward Dudley and faces him and Elena)

    You had a motive for doing away with Lorraine. The rumors of an affair when she was a student could prove not only embarrassing but fatal to your career. But nothing was ever documented and Lorraine was well out of your hair now that she was working for Hartstone.

Dudley: I thought it was Abigail. There was no affair. It was always just a rumor. Sir James..............

Constable Barcroft: Never mind........... I know you didn't do it. Her murder would only convince people of your guilt.

(He moves to Doctor Sullivan. Sullivan tries to stand but is restrained by Maryanne.)

Barcroft: You tend to tipple too much. You should really control that. I don't know if you recognized Lorraine in that chair. You've had a bad time dealing with the Hartstones since the death of their son.

Maryanne: He died after a serious auto accident. No one could have saved him. There was never any malpractice.

Barcroft: Yes I know .... It would be difficult to prove ... if not impossible. You doctors get away with alot...
....
Besides we know you were going to retire from practice in order to run the new institute.......
Your drinking might even be an advantage in that setting.
Killing Abigail certainly would be a stupid and unnecessary act on either of your parts. Besides Sir James would hardly select this forum to have Abigail make such a charge.

(Barcroft circles slowly toward McGuire. John Watts follows slowly.)

We have a bit of a problem with you Mr. McGuire. We have investigated your previous difficulties.

Mcguire: That's old hat! It's all been done before.

Henrietta: He was cleared!

Barcroft: We know..... By your brother............ But the problem is more current. A rather large sum of money has been unaccounted for during the recent building program. In a review of the books at the bank the theft has been carefully covered up.

McGuire: I don't run the bank. I wouldn't have access to those books, It must be Hartstone.

Barcroft: No. The money was an overcharge to the suppliers with you pocketing the difference. The books were handled by Lorraine. She was your accomplice in this scheme. Sir James was about to expose you tonight. You killed Lorraine to throw suspicion elsewhere. You recognized her immediately when she reached for the brandy and saw your opportunity.

(McGuire stands and draws a weapon aiming at Barcroft. With a swift stroke he is disarmed by Wattts who throws him to the floor recovering the gun and points it at him.)

Sir James: No John.... it's not worth it. He will have a long time in prison to contemplate this night. BARCROFT MAKE THE ARREST!

(All the actors leave except Sir James. He gathers a music stand from offstage left and his baton. He slowly moves to stage right. He taps the stand and raises his arms to conduct. But there is no music. He repeats the gestures to no avail He drops his arms grasps the music stand with one hand and lowers his head in his other hand. After a beat the lights go off)

THE END

LAW AND DISORDER

A PLAY IN TWO ACTS

BY BERNARD GARDNER

*(The setting is contemporary in a large teaching
University affiliated hospital)*

CAST IN ORDER OF APPEARANCE

Corpse Dr. Sal Pecorino
Maid Mary Sullivan
Detective Stan Spade
Doctor Jan Watson (crime scene specialist)
Detective Dick Charles (and Asta)
Gloria Pecorino
Doctor George Blackburn (Chief of Medicine)
Doctor Henry Whitehead (Chief of Biochemistry)
Doctor Ross Jones (Chief of Surgery)
Doctor Tricia LaRue (Director of Gerontology)
Doctor Rodney Bedford (President of the University)
Accordionist
Joey (three fingers) Casella
Vito Santorino
Bodyguards 1 and 2
Vincent Farina
Rose Lipschutz
Terry Mason
Della Boulevard
Steno Ginger Snappy
Judge Howard Cheatham
Jury dancers
Ham Burger (District Attorney)
Oliver Twist (world's greatest magician)

ACT I
SCENE 1

(The scene is set in an office. The desk is downstage, partially hiding a male body lying on the floor. A large chair is upstage center with its back to the audience. Stage left has a table with two bottles of whiskey and several glasses, two of them containing a small quantity of liquid. Several chairs are placed about, overturned. Only the corpse's legs are visible. The backdrop should contain some bookshelves. On the desk are a stethoscope, notepads, pens, and a sphygmomanometer with cuff. The maid's voice is heard off-stage.)

Maid: *(Offstage)* Who the hell locked this stupid door..... *(she bangs her pail on the floor and enters carrying a vacuum cleaner, mop and pail. She slams the pail down connects the vacuum cleaner cord and begins to vacuum.)*
What a freaking mess!..........*(she looks at the body)* Hey .... Why'd ya lock the stupid door..........ye know it's my cleaning day.....*(she kicks the leg of the corpse)* Move yer ass. How the hell am I gonna vacuum?..........Okay..........*(she begins to vacuum around the body)* Ye gonna lie there all day?..........*(she walks up toward the head, bends down to look and utters a scream. She races offstage kicking over the bucket and screaming "It's murder..........It's murder..........")* *(lights off)*

SCENE 2

(The setup is the same except yellow police tape surrounds the area of the murder haphazardly. Two CSI persons are dusting everything in sight for clues. The forensic specialist is taking pictures of everything including the audience. The upstage chair is now facing the audience. The two detectives assigned to the case enter stage right. They put on latex gloves. One immediately gets stuck to the yellow tape twisting it up and fouling the crime scene. He has to remove a glove to escape.)

Stan Spade: Well doc what's the story here..........We're Spade and Charles assigned to this one.

Doctor Watson: It's a bit of a mess. The victim is Doctor Sal Pecorino. Apparently struck on the head with a bottle of Kettle One. Been dead about two hours...........

Dick Charles: Was there a suicide note?..........

Spade: Who discovered the body?

Watson: The cleaning lady. Apparently the door was locked from the inside. She used a pass key to get in. No one was here but the corpse. She knocked over her pail when she raced out..........Hysterical.......... Died....around six AM

Spade: No bucket jokes Dicky..........Not another one of those closed room cases!..........Find any thread going through the keyhole to the latch?

Charles: I told you it was suicide.

Watson: Couldn't hit yourself hard enough..........Dick. ....We're dusting everything..........

Spade: Those bottles or glasses been used?

Watson:	A bottle of Scotch and one of Bourbon partially used but the bottles and glasses wiped clean.
Charles:	Partially used?..........
Spade:	Dicky get away from the booze..........we're on duty. ....ANY SIGN OF A BLACK BIRD?????????????????????

(At this moment Gloria Pecorino enters. She is covered in yellow tape and walks over to the body. She is in hysterics.)

Gloria:	What happened to my darling? Who did this terrible thing? Why are you standing there? Go and catch somebody..........Did you find the will???
Spade:	Lady you're screwing up the crime scene!
Gloria:	Somebody screwed up my husband!
Spade:	Try to be calm. Your husband was murdered. We're still getting the facts together.
Charles:	We're very sorry..........
Gloria:	What are you sorry about? You didn't have to live with him for twenty years!
Spade:	Were there problems between you two???
Gloria:	The usual problems..........sex and money.......... Forget it! If I wanted to kill him I'd of done it years ago.
Spade:	Was he cheating on you?
Gloria:	He cheated on everybody..........Go and find out for yourself.

Spade: Did he have any enemies?

Gloria: Enemies???..........No..........It's just that all his friends hated him!

Charles: Did he ever fall down and hit himself in the head with a Vodka bottle?

Watson: Quit it Dicky..........You're gonna have to do a little work. It was murder.

Gloria: Well you should have a long investigation..........

Spade: Did he ever collect BIRD STATUES????

(Lights out)

SCENE 3

(The scene is set in a cafeteria style lunchroom. At a large table center stage are four faculty members eating lunch. There are trays and plates and silverware on the table.)

Dr. George Blackburn: *(internist)* Congratulations Henry. We heard the news this morning. You were named as winner of the Nobel Prize in Medicine. What a phenomenal achievement! When did you write that paper? I don't remember seeing it on your CV.

Dr. Henry Whitebird: (biochemistry) They woke me up at three AM to give me the news. I'd rather sleep..........I can't remember EVER writing that paper. Must be 30 years ago. Probably one of my post docs. ....who shall remain nameless..........I don't even remember the experiments. I guess the co-winners mentioned it in their bibliographies. I keep wracking my mind but I'll be damned..........

Dr. Ross Jones: (surgeon) Don't be so modest Henry.

Dr. Tricia LaRue: (geriatrics) Yes.....Be more like Ross. No worry about modesty in the Surgery Department. How's your golf game Ross?

Dr. Jones: Shot a seventy eight yesterday.

Dr. LaRue: I believe in Gardner's Rule. "NEVER GO TO A SURGEON WITH A LOW HANDICAP."

Dr. Jones: Very funny!

Blackburn: Did you hear about the dinner at the Bedfords?

Jones: It was a riot. President Bedford is trying to recruit Simon Goldberg from the NIH to become the new dean. So he set up a dinner for him and invited the tenured Jewish professors.

Blackburn: Yeah..........Jew night at the Bedfords

Jones: As usual there was plenty to drink but hors d'oeuvres consisted of a few peanuts. Some of the guests were starving when the dinner bell rang..........And guess what they served..........!

LaRue: I can't wait to hear.

Jones: A huge baked ham..........brought it out on a tray and set it down squarely in front of Goldberg.

(All laugh)

Whitebird: He loves his Bourbon..........Alice Smith came down from Washington for a site visit on a half million dollar education grant. The committee rode around in a taxi from LaGuardia and got to Brooklyn via the Bronx..........completely bushed. They arrived in Bedford's office at 8 AM.

Blackburn: You mean Alice the prude. She hasn't cracked a smile in thirty years.

Whitebird: Well she was smiling when she left his office. He brought out the bourbon and insisted they all have a drink.

Blackburn: They didn't get started on the site visit 'till 10:30. Needless to say we got the grant.

(The two detectives enter, look around and approach the table)

Spade: Good afternoon gentlemen....and lady. My name is Stan Spade and this is my partner Detective Dick Charles. ....I suppose you haven't heard the news yet..........one of your faculty friends has been murdered.

Blackburn: Murdered??? Who..........Where..........

Spade: Dr. Sal Pecorino..........

(Dr. LaRue slumps back in her seat in a faint..........Jones rushes to her with a glass of water. Rodney Bedford enters sees what's going on and takes out a flask.....)

Bedford: Give her some of this. ....good bourbon. What happened????

Whitebird: These two detectives just informed us that Pecorino was murdered this morning.

(LaRue revives)

Spade: Sorry to have caused such a ruckus. We'd like to have some information about the deceased.

Charles: We may need that flask for evidence.

Spade: Forget it Dicky..........

Jones: He was a general practitioner, and pretty much of a pain in the ass. There was a lot of dissension in the faculty due to his shenanigans.

Blackburn: Take it easy Ross. You were the most upset at him.

Jones: Don't point any fingers at me. ....Pecorino introduced a plan here that amounted to fee splitting, in my opinion. He set up a huge emergency center, manned by him and several partners. All cases referred to specialists were to be billed by the center with a charge of 20 to 40 percent of the collection as a billing fee. Some of our specialists were joining to get referrals at the expense of those that refused to join. All of those that joined had their own offices and billing system. Pecorino's was just a way of getting a kickback for the referral.

Blackburn: Well you were pretty pissed that it was destroying your department..........Some of his surgeons apparently signed on. I didn't see what all the fuss was about.

Whitebird: It had some pretty bad effects throughout the faculty and the hospital.

Spade: What was your opinion President Bedford.

Bedford: Well I was concerned about the possibility of adverse publicity..........particularly if the newspapers got hold of the scheme. It certainly looked like a fee splitting scheme. Our board already ordered our lawyers to look into the plan.

LaRue: It was set up as an HMO. Perfectly legal.

Jones: Sure.....What HMO do you know that takes 40% for referral fees??

Bedford: Our in house lawyer felt the same. Pecorino already instituted a suit against the hospital for restraint of trade. We had opinions that this was very irregular..........

Charles: Sounds pretty messy. Dr. LaRue what is your specialty.

LaRue:	Geriatrics. I see many patients in nursing homes and rehab centers.
Charles:	I bet patients sit up and take notice when you walk into the room.
Whitebird:	That's not all that gets up.....when she walks into a room!
Blackburn:	She specializes in ED in the elderly. ....She has a treatment that doesn't require Viagra.
Spade:	Who are named as defendants in the suit?
Bedford:	Well ....the hospital board, Blackburn, Jones, I, and our legal council.
Spade:	I guess Dr. Jones you and Pecorino didn't much care for one another..........How did Pecorino finance the opening of the Emergency Center? It must cost a lot to do that.
Blackburn:	Well the rumor is that he had connections that put the money up.
Charles:	Connections???
Blackburn:	You know..........He was connected..........His lawyer Santorini would know.
Spade:	Well if you mean Vito Santorini we got the picture..........Ok thanks for your time. By the way where were you all at six AM this morning?
Blackburn:	Having an egg MacMuffm. Don't know if anyone would remember me.....
Jones:	In my office preparing for rounds..........by myself. My first case was canceled so I had some extra time..........

LaRue: Saying goodbye to a friend..........

Whitebird: Trying to get back to sleep..........after the Nobel notification..........

Charles: Don't play games with us..........

Bedford: No he really means it..........He's a Nobel prize winner..........I was in my office..........I don't think anyone would notice..........By the way I'm setting up a party for Whitebird next Saturday night..........You're all invited.

(He walks off)

Jones: *(To the others)* YOU'D BETTER PACK SOME SANDWICHES..........

(Lights out)

SCENE 4

(The setting is an Italian Restaurant. At a central table Joey Threefingers Casella is seated eating from several dishes with a napkin dangling from his neck. A bottle of red wine and a single glass is next to his dish. Vito Santorino is seated next to him. Two body guards are standing behind him and off to one side is the waiter. The scene opens with an accordion player playing the full "Godfather" music.)

Casella: I love that song. Donny make me a record of that..........I'll play it in the shower.

Santorino: Yeah it's beautiful..........

(A man enters and approaches the table)

Bodyguard 1:   Don't get too close!

Vincent Farina: Don Three fingers..........

Casella: Stupedo.....Don't address me by my disability.

Farina: Sorry Don Joey..........I'm here to plead a case..........A man has disrespected my only daughter.

Casella: Sounds serious!..........What happened?

Farina: This man asked my permission to take my daughter out. I said ok. They went to a dinner

93

and a concert. He bought her flowers. So after the concert my daughter naturally asked if they could go to his apartment for drinks and fun.

Casella: Your daughter wanted to go to his apartment??

Farina: And he refused. He said on a first date she should go home. This is gross disrespect.

Casella: You got a picture of your daughter? ....*(He looks at a photograph)*..........My god..........she certainly looks like your daughter..........I'll take care of it. For you....as a payment of respect.......... you will deliver to me a dozen Cannelonis from your bakery every Friday.

Farina: Thank you ...Thank you... *(He kisses the Don's hand and leaves. Casella turns to one of his bodyguards)*

Casella: Find that guy and give him a coupla hundred bucks. He must have had a strong stomach to look at that face over dinner..........(he turns to Santorini) So what happened?..........Who the f—k killed the bastard..........How'my gonna get my money back?

Santorino: We're looking into it. Somebody bopped him with a Vodka bottle.

Casella: It's not that broad Trixie?.....Nah.....She had nothin' to gain. Unless Gloria found out he was bangin' her.

Santorino: I don't think so. If anything his WIFE might finish him off..........But there's nothing being whispered around about a contract..........

Casella: So where do we stand?

Santorino: I'll get someone to take over the Emergency

Offices. We lose on the kick-back plan. ....
and of course the suit against the hospital is
defunct..........but you'll be okay..........

Casella: You see to it!

(At this moment Charles and Spade enter stage right and approach the table)

Casella: Oh shit..........if it ain't the Bobsy Twins..........

Charles: Hello Joey. Drinkin' any Vodka recently?..........*(he picks up the wine bottle)*

Spade: Leave the bottle alone Dicky..........Heard about Pecorino?..........They say he was a friend of yours..........Hello Vito..........Just give him the news?

Casella: A friend of mine?

Spade: Yeah..........connected so they say.

Casella: Everybody's connected!..........He don't even have the right name. His family is named after a CHEESE!

Charles: I suppose you didn't front for that Emergency Center?

Casella: That's my business. You don't think I'd waste good Vodka on that bum???

Santorino: I don't think I want my client to answer anymore questions..........You guys are barking in the wrong pen..........Go do some more legwork..........you might find better prospects.

Spade: Burger is pushing to close this out.

Santorino: Don't try to close it out here. My client had nothing to do with that murder. He needed to have Pecorino alive..........Try that surgeon.......... what's his name..........Jones.

Spade: We may be back

(Casella flips his hand at them. The accordion player starts a little Tarantella as the detectives stalk out ...lights out)

SCENE 5

(The scene is set in Jones' office. He is seated at his desk as his mother Rose Lipschutz enters. She is wearing a beautiful gown, fur jacket and jewelry.)

Jones: Ma what are you doing here? You're supposed to be in Miami.

Rose: I know you're in trouble. I'm doing what any mother would do. I came to help.

Jones: I'm being indicted for a murder I didn't have anything to do with..........But how did you know?..........Are you a medium now?..........

Rose: *(With her chest out hands on her hips she poses)* Sonny boy...........DO I LOOK LIKE A MEDIUM?..........A mother knows. ....I gave up a good Canasta tournament to come up here from Miami.

Jones: Those guys still running after you down there?

Rose: Baby..........Where I live those guys don't run anymore..........THEY HOBBLE...........I've got two hobbling after me now.. They may need assisted living ....but I don't need any help.

Jones: You're really enjoying life since the divorce and you got all that money.

Rose: After 20 years with your father I'm still recuperating.....Honey......Why'd you change your name? What was wrong with Dr. Ronald Lipschutz.

Jones: Lipschutz just doesn't make it in academic surgery..........Jones is a lot better.

Rose: Well it doesn't interfere with MY getting noticed..........

Jones: Ma..........Nothing would ever interfere with your getting anything!

Rose: Got a lawyer?

Jones: I'm still looking for a good one. I'd better hurry.

Rose: Don't make a move! I've got the perfect solution. An old friend of mine Terry Mason is the best defense lawyer around. I'll see him with you.... he'll be perfect.

Jones: I hope your right. I'll need all the help I can get. He's a big time attorney. I hope he has the time to do this..........How well did you know him?

Rose: Sonny..........I guarantee HE WON'T TURN US DOWN.

(Lights out)

SCENE 6

(As the scene opens we're in Terry Mason's office. Della Boulevard is sitting in his lap taking dictation.)

Mason: Della take a letter..........

Della: To whom are we sending this?..........

Mason: It doesn't matter. I just love giving you dictation..........

Della: I know..........I can tell..........By the way you have an appointment with Rose Lipschutz this morning. ....*(she gets up and moves to the front of the desk)*

Mason: You mean Gypsy Rose Lipschutz. I haven't seen her in years..........I guess her surgeon son is in trouble about that murder..........

Della: Just don't stand up when she comes in..........She might think you were glad to see her!

(Rose storms in dragging her son.)

Rose: Terry ...sweetheart..........So happy to see you. And Della..........I see you finally made it..........personal secretary that is..........

Mason: Rose.....still as perky as ever. You're a

wonder..........What can I do for you? and Doctor Lipschutz..........

Jones: Jones..........it's Jones.

Mason: Of course.

Rose: That stupid DA ..what's his name...Burger is putting my son on trial for the murder at the hospital.

Mason: I've been following that case..........Della leave Dr. Jones alone.

Della: Just trying to put him at ease..........

Mason: I'll get all the details..........Of course I'll take the case. It should be interesting...I understand he was killed in a locked room.

Jones: Yes.....and there are plenty of people that wanted him dead..........I wasn't one of them, although we had our differences.

Mason: I'll have my investigator work on this today. (He stands up to take Rose's hand and bid her goodbye)

Rose: I knew you wouldn't let me down. Thanks a million Terry. If there's anything I can do.......... Well it is certainly heartening to see how glad you were to see me!

(Lights out..........END OF ACT I)

ACT II

(The action takes place in the courtroom. The Judge's desk is center stage with the witness chair to the left. Six chairs are lined up on stage left for the jury. Two tables are for the defense - downstage right and prosecution downstage left. At the right center stage nine additional chairs are set up for witnesses. A stenographer sits in front of the judge. Various papers and notes are on the desks. When the lights go on the prosecutor Burger is seated as are Mason and Della and Jones. The jury is not yet sworn and the Judge is not seated. The witnesses include the maid, Spade, Casella, LaRue, Rose, Whitebird, Blackburn, Bedford and Twist.)

Steno: Everybody rise.

(Judge Howard Cheatham enters, takes his seat and everyone sits down. He stands up to adjust his chair and everyone rises, he sits down and everyone sits down. He repeats this once more.)

Cheatham: I love this job..........Ok lets get the jury in.

Steno: Will the jury enter please.

(The jury dances in (music to be decided) and finally take their seats)

Cheatham: Great show..........Okay Burger You go first..........
                   And skip the opening. We know you think he's
                   guilty..........Let's get out of here for lunch. Call
                   your first witness.

Burger: I call Miss Mary Sullivan.

(Mary Sullivan, the maid, walks to the witness stand. mutters She is dressed to the hilt with jewelry, fancy dress and a hat with flowers. The steno swears her in.)

Steno: Do you swear to tell the truth and stop wearing that stupid hat any more?

Maid: I guess so!

Cheatham: What the hell did you have her swear to? Ok Proceed.

Burger: Miss Sullivan..........You are the maid assigned to the offices of the deceased?

Maid: Yes sir I clean regularly every day. I scrub down the floors, dust the desk and chairs, arrange the furniture..........

Cheatham: Do you do windows?..........Here take my card.

Burger: You found the body?..........Was the door open when you went in?

Maid: Why no sir. It was locked tight. I had to use my passkey to get in. It was locked from the inside. It was a horrible experience..........Horrible..........

Burger: Was there anyone else in the room?

Maid: Not that I seen..........Nobody.

Cheatham: How're you gonna get around that one Ham?

Burger: Don't worry Judge I got that one figured out. This'l be the prosecution of the century!..........No further questions.

Cheatham: Ok Mason you go.

Mason:	I have just one question. Miss Sullivan did you notice anything unusual about the room?
Maid:	No...I don't....think..........Now that you mention it ...there was something funny about the large chair behind the desk..........
Mason:	Thank you ....No further questions.
Burger:	Call detective Stan Spade to the stand.
Steno:	Hi Stan. Had any parties lately? Do you swear to tell the truth. ....and call me.
Spade:	Sure baby.
Burger:	Were you in charge of the investigation?
Spade:	Yes. The deceased was found lying on his back having died from a blow to the head by a Vodka Bottle. No fingerprints were found besides the deceased. We searched the room looking for clues but nothing showed up..........not even the black bird.
Cheatham:	You're in the wrong movie Spade.
Spade:	The deceased was involved in a questionable operation with an Emergency Center and there were several suits started.
Casella:	I object..........There was nothing questionable..........
Cheatham:	Sit down Joey. You'll get your chance.
Spade:	The hospital was involved and could lose money..........and Jones stood to have his department go under if the suit was won by Pecorino.

Burger:	How do you explain the murder in a locked room?
Spade:	We're working on it. He couldn't have hit himself hard enough ....so suicide was ruled out.
Burger:	Don't worry ....I figured it out for you. That's all.
Mason:	Did you notice anything in the room that seemed out of place?
Spade:	No.
Mason:	Did you find anything in the room that would have placed the defendant there?
Spade:	No..........the killer must have worn gloves.
Mason:	Like you could find in any dollar store!..........No further questions.
Burger:	I call Rodney Bedford to the stand
Steno:	Nice suit. You must be loaded. ....Give me an "I do" Rodney. I'll fill in the rest.....
Bedford:	I do.
Burger:	You are the President of the Medical Center where the deceased had his practice, is that correct?
Bedford:	Yes. You should come up and have a drink with us sometime.
Steno:	I accept!
Cheatham:	Control yourself, Ginger.

Burger: Is it true that the Center and several faculty members were being sued by Pecorino?

Bedford: Yes..........Pecorino had developed a kickback scheme for specialists to whom he referred patients..........taking 40% as billing fees.....we had to stop that..........

LaRue: It was an HMO..........not a scheme

Casella: Yeah an HMO

Jones: Bullocks..........It was a kickback scheme...

LaRue: You were just jealous..you didn't think of it first..........

Rose: Don't you dare call my son jealous..........you..........floozy.

Cheatham: ORDER..........ORDER IN THE COURT......... OR I'LL HAVE YOU SHOT.

(Bedford turns toward the Judge raises his hand. thinks better of it and turns back)

Burger: Who else was named in the suit?

Bedford: Dr. Blackburn, the Hospital Board, our in-house council,..........and the defendant Ross Jones. We were each being sued for two million dollars.

Burger: What would have happened to Jones' practice and position if that suit was successful?

Mason: Objection..........calls for an opinion.

Cheatham: Sustained. Sharpen it up Ham.

Burger:	I suppose you all would have had a tough time..........Never mind.....withdrawn. No further questions.
Mason:	No questions at this time. I reserve the right to recall this witness.
Cheatham:	Sounds guilty to me! Let's all go home early. Della if you get any closer to Mason I'll call the vice squad..........
Della:	We're just consulting.
Burger:	I call Tricia LaRue to the stand.
Steno:	Do you swear to tell the truth and keep your legs crossed at all times?
LaRue:	I do.
Cheatham:	Just be at ease Dr. LaRue. Here's my card in case you require ...legal advice.
Burger:	You are on the faculty at the Medical Center, isn't that true?
LaRue:	Yes.
Burger:	Were you familiar with all the participants in the suit.
LaRue:	I was familiar with everybody at the Center.
Bedford:	I'll say..........
Cheatham:	Quiet!
Burger:	Tell the Jury the circumstances of the suit.

LaRue: Well Dr. Pecorino opened an Emergency Center and a number of specialists joined with him in order to get referrals. He offered to bill for their services and charge a regular billing fee which was a percentage of the collections. This upset those specialists who were not invited to join. When the administration heard about the deal they sensed competition and reported him to the medical board which voted to take action. As a result Dr. Pecorino instituted a suit.

Burger: What was the feeling of the defendant?

LaRue: Not Bad!..........I mean he was instrumental in labeling this as a kick-back scheme. As a result he was a prime target.

Burger: Your witness.

Della: Keep your distance Terry

Mason: Dr. LaRue, Aren't you also known as Trixie?

LaRue: Some people call me that.

Mason: And weren't you seeing Pecorino intimately, in fact having a torrid affair with him?

Gloria: So that's the little trick he was playing with.

Casella: At a girl Trixie..........That freekin' cheesehead.

LaRue: We saw each other.

Mason: And didn't you get your opinions about the suit from the deceased?

LaRue: We discussed it.

Mason:	One other question..........Did you ever witness the deceased drinking Bourbon?
LaRue:	Bourbon? He'd rather die..........He was strictly a Vodka person.
Mason:	Maybe he did..........No further questions.
Burger:	At this time I call to the stand Rose Lipschutz.
Rose:	I'm not going..........I don't like that guy.....he's trying to hurt my Ronald.
Bedford:	Ronald??????
Steno:	C'mon Mommy..........you better get up here pronto. *(Rose goes up to the stand.)* Raise your hand baby..........like to see the jewels..........Who was your divorce lawyer?
Rose:	I do.
Burger:	Just one question. Did you or your former husband ever buy Ronald a magician set?
Rose:	Why yes..........he played with it all the time..........I'm not answering any more questions! I am standing on the first Commandment
Cheatham:	What the hell is the first Commandment?
Rose:	A mother never hurts her baby boy!
Cheatham:	Ham..........You'd better have a good reason for asking stupid questions.
Burger:	You'll see
Mason:	No questions.

Burger: I call to the stand Oliver Twist!

(Oohs and aahs in the crowd)

Steno: Can I have your autograph?..........and phone
                number. You don't have to tell the truth to
                me..........lie a little..........

Cheatham: Control yourself Ginger.....

Twist: I do.

Burger: Are you also known as the world's most famous
                and talented magician?

Twist: I guess so.

Burger: So modest. Aren't you known in magazines, on
                television for your abilities in appearing and
                disappearing?

Twist: Yes.

Burger: Among all your magical activities didn't you
                levitate..........And make tigers disappear?

Twist: Yes.

Burger: And didn't you walk through solid objects..........
                IN FACT DIDN'T YOU ONCE WALK
                THROUGH THE GREAT WALL OF
                CHINA?????????????

Twist: Yes. That episode was documented on television.

Burger: And although you are the greatest couldn't

another magician, with practice learn to do the same thing?

Twist: I......suppose it's possible.

Burger: And isn't it true that if you could walk through a wall..........a closed door would be a cinch for a magician.

Twist: Well...I suppose so.....

Burger: There's the testimony..........That's how it was done. The murderer killed Pecorino and simply left through the closed door! The prosecution rests!

Cheatham: Sounds good to me..........Let's eat!

Mason: Hold on judge. I get a chance here.

Cheatham: Okay Mason but make it snappy.

Mason: How many years of training and practice did you have before you could walk through a wall?

Twist: Many years..........probably 15 or 20.

Mason: So how could a surgeon after 15 years of training find the time to do this? Never mind.......... Withdrawn..........No further questions..........I call to the stand Gloria Pecorino.

(Gloria dressed in black with a veil, goes to the stand)

Steno: Sorry about your hubby..........Where'd you get the outfit?..........

Gloria: Bergdorf..........Don't be sorry for me babe..........I found the will! ...I do.

Mason: Mrs. Pecorino, didn't you suspect that your husband was playing around?

Gloria: Always..........It was a habit with him.

Mason: And wouldn't that lead to violence on your part?

Gloria: The only violence came when he tried to play around with me!

Mason: You didn't like your husband did you?

Gloria: It was a normal marriage.

Mason: Couldn't you have gone to his office and killed him?

Gloria: Are you nuts? Get up at six AM?..........If I wanted to kill him I'd have done it at a reasonable hour.

Mason: But you were the sole beneficiary of the estate. You stood to gain the most from his death.

Gloria: I didn't need to kill him to use his money. I knew he liked to play around. A few good credit cards and I didn't complain. Besides I had a few coals in the fire.

Mason: I see...........No further questions at this time.

Burger: You look terrific in that outfit. No questions at this time..........I may have a few later!

Mason: I call Dr. George Blackburn to the stand.

Steno: You married George?..........State your name address and phone number..........

Blackburn: I do.

Mason: You're the director of medicine, isn't that so?

Blackburn: Yes.

Mason: And as such you were the department chief over the deceased.

Blackburn: Yes that's correct.

Mason: You were a named defendant in the suit.

Blackburn: Yes I was. But I didn't see anything wrong with the plan. Doctors can practice any way they see fit.

Mason: But the hospital board had opinions stating that it was akin to fee splitting. Isn't that detrimental to the practice of medicine? Didn't you take this line in order to protect yourself in case Pecorino won? Didn't you meet with him to give him your support so he would drop you from the suit?

Blackburn: I had a department to run. The suit was interfering with that.

Mason: So medical ethics had no place in your department.

Blackburn: There was a difference of opinion..........

Mason: But you had several outside opinions on this that also considered it fee splitting..........

Blackburn: That would be settled in the suit.

Mason: No further questions for this..........doctor.

Burger: No questions.

Mason:	I call Joey Casella to the stand.

(Casella rises and he and two body guards approach the witness stand. Some Godfather music is heard.)

Cheatham:	Only one person please.
Casella:	I ain't goin' nowhere without my friends!
Cheatham:	Oh..........okay..........but only one of you sits.
Steno:	No use swearing you in..........
Casella:	I do.
Mason:	Mr. Casella you spend most of your time at the pinochle club don't you?
Casella:	What!.....Are you a poker freak?
Mason:	And aren't you an associate of known criminals....A made family member?
Casella:	I have a large family..........If any of them are crooks I don't know about it. What are your family members so clean?
Mason:	Don't you sometimes lend money?
Casella:	I invest!
Mason:	Didn't you finance Pecorino's emergency center? And didn't you stand to lose money if the suit failed?
Casella:	I never lose money. Why would I kill him?.......... We didn't lose the suit..........and that schlemiel said he had something up his sleeve that would guarantee the hospital would settle.

Mason: Did he tell you what that was?

Casella: We never discussed it

Mason: It doesn't matter..........I know what it was..........
                     Nothing further.

Burger: No questions.

Mason: At this time I recall Rodney Bedford to the stand.

Cheatham: You're still under oath such as it is.

Mason: Is there anyone that could corroborate your
                     whereabouts at the time of the murder?

Bedford: No no one saw me.

Mason: In your previous position as president weren't you
                     cautioned about your drinking habits?

Bedford: I don't recall..........

Mason: Isn't it true Doctor that in 2004 you were fired
                     from your job as University dean?

Bedford: That was a political decision.

Mason: And didn't you take a sabbatical for six months of
                     rehabilitation???

Bedford: I needed the rest.

Mason: Isn't it true that you had a meeting with Pecorino
                     the morning he was killed?

Bedford: I..........

Mason: Wasn't that half filled bottle of bourbon one that you brought to that meeting?

Bedford: That's possible..........Maybe I left it from another meeting.

Mason: Didn't Pecorino threaten to disclose your drinking problem to the papers if you didn't push for settlement of the suit?..........You got angry and hit him with the Vodka bottle.

Burger: He's no magician. ....he couldn't walk through the door.

Mason: Bring in the chair!

(Della goes the side and leads two men in with the chair. It is placed with its back to the audience.)

Burger: It's another Mason stunt! Judge I object..........

Cheatham: You'd better have a good reason for this playacting!

Mason: Doctor Bedford would you please sit in this chair.

(Bedford sits in the chair scrunched down so he could not be seen from behind)

Mason: Mary Sullivan testified that the chair was out of place. It was turned away from the body. The murderer was in the room when the maid came in. When she ran out of the room he simply got up, turned the chair around and walked out. Didn't you Doctor Bedford?

Bedford: He was trying to ruin the Medical Center with his scheme. When he refused my bourbon offering..........I lost it..........

Cheatham: Okay Burger Make yourself useful once..........

(Burger rises and handcuffs Bedford...........Lights out)

THE END

IT STAYS HERE

A new original play

by Bernard Gardner

CAST (in order of appearance)

Anne Bonham
John Bonham
Maria Snyder
Harvey Snyder
Tony Petrilla
Alice Petrilla
Minnie Salvatore
Madame Zapotnik
Three Fingers Louie
Reservation Clerk
Belhop
Head Waiter
Show Performer(s)
Nervous Crapshooter
Personal Shopper
Doreen Sullivan
Waiter
Madame Lavoisier
Eddie Burns

The play is set in the present at a golfing community in Florida.

ACT I

SCENE 1 *(The home of John and Anne Bonham.)*

Anne:	I just don't understand you....... Why do you have to go this week.
John:	I explained already............. The other couples set this up. It's the only date available.
Anne:	I can't believe it ....you know I'm playing for the club Championship this weekend. How could you agree??..........I won't go!
John:	The rooms are half price. We get a hundred bucks back for the plane. It's a junket.
Anne:	Sure and you'll lose a thousand at the crap tables.... It's no use...... When was the last time you thought about what I want. Where's the partnership in this deal???............. I'm not going. ....You go................... and you'd better not have a good time.............
John:	It's just the ladies' final....................... It's not like it's the men's.
Anne:	Oh Reeeeally................Your chauvinism is showing.....Pull that line on your friends.......................
John:	Look I didn't mean it that way............You'll have another crack at it next year...........

Anne: You're getting annoying now.............

John: C'mon Annie.......... We'll have a ball

Anne: It's something we could do anytime...................
                 And don't plan on having a ball when you get
                 back home! ....Is that extra cot still in the
                 garage?

John: Please don't be that way...............I promise to
                 always put the toilet seat down .... I'll put the
                 new paper on the roll.................

*(John walks over to her and tries to reach for her shoulder. Anne turns
slowly away to avoid him)*

Anne: Your comedic talents are leaving me
                 cold...............I resent your attitude and
                 selfishness... Why are you so nonchalant about
                 this?

John: I'm just trying to calm you down. You're taking
                 this too seriously...

Anne: Boy... You're just not getting it............ Not now
                 ....and not when you get back.

(Lights out ....and on)

(...At the home of the Snyders)

Maria: What a terrific idea. Four days in Vegas. I'll get
                 tickets for the shows. We have comps for two of
                 them already.

Harvey: Now don't book up all our time. We'll need some
                 time to gamble.

Maria: How about eating............. do we have to skip that???? Or maybe we can fit that in on your way to the John.

Harvey: Don't be a wise-ass!............We'll get to some great restaurants. But we're committed to a certain number of hours at the tables.

Maria: How much time is a certain amount??

Harvey: Three hours a day................Green chips.

Maria: I'm worried about that............You know you've had trouble at the tables before............Three hours............You could lose a fortune in three hours.

I'm not going through this again............It almost cost our marriage last time.

Harvey: I know........ But I'm in full control now..... When I left treatment they told me that short exposures would be okay.

Maria: I hope so. Four days can be a long time.......... Please don't go overboard

Harvey: We formed a syndicate. Each of the three of us puts in a thousand bucks and we keep any loser alive as long as possible. We use our own systems with no exotic bets unless we're way ahead. On a cold table we're out after 10 minutes. We'll have a coffee or something and try again later.

Maria: Sounds okay..........You'll probably be on a caffeine high for most of the trip....................Three thousand ought to last at least an hour.

Harvey: Don't be funny. We're all experienced players..................... What a great idea . Who thought this up??

Maria: Alice made the arrangements. She used to
be a travel agent and knew the guy that
arranges the junkets. ....Three finger Louie or
something......... She said he was a collector ....
....I don't know what he
collects.

Harvey: A great idea..............Absolutely great. ....What
time do we leave?

Maria: The bus to the airport will pick us up at 8:30
in the parking lot. Then we're off. Four days of
shows,.................... shopping............I'll shop
while you're shooting craps.

Harvey: Yeah............You'll spend more on shopping than
we.

can lose at the tables

Maria: I'll drink to that!

(Lights out ....then on)

*(We are at the home of the Petrillas.   Tony and Alice are standing and
Alice's mother is seated at a table drinking coffee and reading a paper. She
is wearing an old smock with her hair in curlers))*

Tony: This should be our cheapest vacation. We've got
comps for shows and two restaurants.

Alice: Two restaurants????...You mean breakfast buffets,
don't you??

Minnie: I see el cheapo has struck again.

Tony: Look, you can eat enough at those to last most of
the day. I'll buy some booze when we land so we
can party in our room.

Alice: Some vacation. ....You sure you want me to come?

Minnie: Yeah take me instead. I promise not to eat anything.

Tony: Cut it out Ma..............You're one step from the old age home now.

Minnie: Yeah and you lose my rent? Fat chance you'll give that up.

Alice: Ma be nice........I really want to go on this trip.

Tony: Baby.I love you ...but.........Take it easy on the slots Huh............

Alice: I got a system...........You tip the change lady ten bucks and she tells you which slots are ready to pay off.

Minnie: How has that worked out now that everyone uses credit cards........................... Must get the change ladies pretty pissed to see their jobs go down the tubes.

Alice: You know I have noticed a change in my luck lately.

Tony: Yeah you got creamed the last few times.......Listen baby..Take it easy on the sweets also................

Minnie: Oh now he's a diet doctor............

Alice: Are you hinting that I'm fat???

Tony: No no.............I love you that way............. Just.. You been guzzling the deserts lately..........It's not good for your heart.

Minnie: A cardiologist too??????????????????

Alice: Mom take it easy. ....Yeah I know..............
you're interested in my health.

Tony: That three fingered Louie gets me nervous.........
creepy sort of guy..........

Alice: You only have to see him if you don't settle your
markers before you leave the hotel. ....He'll
coming knocking at your door.

Tony: No worry about that. Our syndicate will triumph!
...........It only needs one of us to get lucky.....

Minnie: Better leave your jewelry at home.

Tony: Ma one more crack and I'm shipping you to your
son's house! See how you like it with your ditsy
daughter-in-law...................Stop worrying babe
we'll be fine.

Alice: Seems I've heard that before.

(Lights out)

SCENE 2

(We are in the home of Madame Zabotnik. She is seated at a table with a crystal ball and is reading a set of Tarot Cards. She is wearing a turban clanging jewelry heavy makeup and a blouse with wide flared long sleeves and a skirt with a wide red sash. On a table or cupboard behind her are vials and bottles. We will need to decorate the room. There is a knock at the door.)

Mme Z: Come in ...Come in.... Enter these hallowed halls...........

(Anne Bonham slowly wanders in. She looks around and takes a few steps toward Mme Z.)

Mme Z: Don't be afraid my child...........Come tell me your desire...........A reading of the cards..........a tale of the future........Some impending event

(She takes Anne's hand)

Mme Z: Oh.. Oh   ... A husband problem.............Or a lover perhaps.????..........

Anne: I wish..........No you got it right the first time.

Mme Z: Another lady????...............Perhaps a secretary?..............**We'll turn her food to worms**...............She won't eat for months..............

Anne: No, not yet. He's taking a trip to Vegas ...... without me.

Mme Z:	AHA...............It **is** his secretary..............**We'll take all the vowels off her computer**..........She'll be fired in a week.
Anne:	No, no, He's going with our friends. I'm afraid he'll do..............something.....Being on the loose. You know..............Vegas and all............. Oh I don't know.
Mme Z:	**I** know. You cannot trust a man.........They weel stray at the first opportunity. They think with their.................**Hormones.**
Anne:	That will affect our relationship........Which right now is sinking fast.........I just wish ....
Mme Z:	**Wait.......I have a special potion.**..............It weel shrivel up his ....you know...................... ....private parts for a week..... But there is one possible complication...............
Anne:	A complication?
Mme Z:	Yes.....**Kidney failure**............But I theenk that is treatable.
Anne:	No I don't want to hurt him. Not yet anyhow...............Oh I feel so foolish coming here and taking your time...........I don't even know if there will be a problem.
Mme Z:	In Vegas?? I can guarantee there will be a problem............Men are guided by a single force............An **uncontrollable** urge...........
Anne:	I know.........If he did that............I would know when he came back......I don't think I could ever ....be the same with him.
Mme Z:	**Yes** You are right. Marital bonds need constant

reinforcing.........They are made of gossamer.........
easily torn apart.

Anne: I'm not certain ...but I think I need help.

Mme Z: I understand...........My dear, do not fret..... I am
here to help with this problem.............Let me
see........................ There is one solution.   It is
very powerful ....I have never used it ....
but my twin sister in Vegas knows about it..........

(She turns to look at her vials and bottles. She takes one and hands it to Anne.)

Mme Z: Tonight before he leaves have a drink with
him..........Champagne works best. Add the
contents of this vial to his drink. He will travel the
straight and narrow for you.

Anne: I hope there are no lasting side effects....

(She sits down, writes a check.. and hands it to Mme Z. Who takes it, kisses it and deposits it.)

Mme Z: **My dear a satisfied customer is good for business.**

(As Anne rises to leave)

Mme Z: Can I do anything to help with your golf
game???? Give your challenger a little arthritis
perhaps??????????????

Anne: No thanks ....It needs to be an honest
game.................Although.......my
putting......................

(LIGHTS OUT)

SCENE 3

(John and Anne are on stage. A bottle of champagne and two glasses are on the table. John turns ad walks over to the CD player and puts on some romantic music. Anne empties the vial into John's glass. He returns. They both drink as they hold hands.............LIGHTS OUT)

SCENE 4

(In the parking lot waiting for the bus. John, Harvey and Maria are waiting with carry-on cases. Tony walks in wheeling his case.)

Harvey: Hi man,.....What a great idea you guys arranged. I love it....

Maria: Yeah we're looking for a terrific time. Anne can't make it so we're all pledged to take care of John............no foolin' around.

John: I don't need watching. I'll be a good boy............. Hey where's Alice.

Tony: She's coming.

(At this time Alice walks on stage with two heavy suitcases on wheels.)

Maria: Oh my God.............We're only going for four days................What are you going to do with all those clothes??????????

Alice: I just don't know what I'm going to wear.......I like to have choices.

Tony: Forget about it..........It's no use...........I gave up arguing with her twenty years ago.

(Three fingered Louie walks in.....)

Louie: **OK folks let's get a move on.**

(LIGHTS OUT   *END OF ACT ONE)*

ACT II
SCENE 1

(In the hotel lobby. They are trying to register. John is not present.. Harvey and Maria are frustrated as Tony and Alice walk on stage......they are dragging the luggage.)

Harvey: They won't have our room ready for three
                 hours..............seems there was a party there last
                 night........they're still waking people up after the
                 ambulance left.

Maria: They need an hour to clear out the cigar
                 smoke............or some kind of smoke.............I
                 think it was cigars.................

(Tony walks in followed by Alice. Both have their luggage)

Harvey: What happened to you guys. I thought you
                 registered already.

Tony: I didn't follow my own advice..........You never
                 take the first room they give you. Always ask for
                 the second room when you register.

Alice: Well we had a choice......Either it was us or the luggage.

Tony: We couldn't fit both into the room...........No wonder
                 it was half price.....they gave us half a room.

(John walks in with his luggage.)

John: Did you know the hotel is undergoing
                 renovations. The jackhammer starts at

six AM. .... Right under my
window........................ But I have a great view
of the parking garage.

Alice: I can't believe they did this.

(Louie Three fingers walks in..........)

Louie: You folks all set??

Alice: It's a disaster!! The rooms are either dirty, small or
on the side with renovations. I thought we had a
guarantee of deluxe rooms....

Louie: Absolutely...........We got deluxe rooms.
However.............. this hotel has extra deluxe,
Super deluxe, and VIP rooms before you get to
the HIGH ROLLER category. Wait here I'll
check out the problem..........

Tony: Yeah..Please... Before we checkout.

*(Louie walks to the check-in desk and converses with the clerk...After a few
minutes he returns.)*

Louie: I got it all solved. You all get two upgrades. You'll
love the rooms.....I guarantee it. Now go and
register they're all ready.

Maria: Thank goodness. I had visions of a total foul up
and a miserable trip home.

(They all go to the desk to fill out the forms..........Louie takes John aside)

Louie: There's one small detail........You gotta give
them four hours a day. I'm sure you won't have
a problem with that.........After all you still got
twenty hours a day to enjoy Vegas.

(Lights out)

SCENE 2

(We are in John's room. He is looking out the window at the view.)

John: Not bad......If you stretch a little bit you can see the strip.....Too bad Anne couldn't be here...... she'll be pissed..... but she'll get over it...........I'll buy her something downstairs.

(At this moment Anne glides on stage............She is wearing a long white gown.)

Anne: I'm getting a present for your bad behavior??......... Can I pick it out??

John: My God.................You made it after all........... How did you manage it??

Anne: No I didn't make it ....I'm playing golf, remember.

John: What are you talking about................You're right here.

Anne: Not really..............

(At this moment there's a knock at the door. A bellhop enters with a tray of ice and a bottle of scotch.............He (she) walks right past Anne............)

Anne: I see you're planning a little partying.

John: No............ I just like a drink before I retire.

Bellhop: Beg pardon sir?..............

John: No just mumbling to myself.

Anne: I see you're getting the hang of things......

John: You have to stop talking to me..............

Bellhop: Sorry sir....Did I say something???

Anne: No he's just confused.

John: **I'm not confused.**

(The bellhop runs offstage......murmuring something about forget the tip)

John: How long is this supposed to go on. Are you going to be all over the hotel?

Anne: No darling.............I will be where you are ....I'll only be around when you think of me.............As often as possible ...I hope..............

John: **Are you real???** ....I must be going nuts...........No one else can see you?

Anne: Darling....I'm not here.........I'm playing golf!

(Anne walks slowly off stage.)

John: I'd better lay off the Scotch...................

(Lights out)

SCENE 3

(They are sitting at a table in the night club. A second table is on stage. Harvey is looking through binoculars)

Tony: You brought binoculars?

Harvey: It's the only way I can see the stage. They rent 'em on the way in. Jeeze how much did you tip that guy??

Tony: I slipped him 10 bucks.

Alice: Ten bucks????...You are living in the dark ages.

John: *(He signals for the head waiter.)* I'll give him another thirty and see if we can get a booth or something closer.

(The Waiter comes over and consults with John who slips him the money. He looks it over and they all get up and traipse around to the other table.)

(The SHOW. The typical Las Vegas show includes a singer and a comedian. For the purposes of the play guest performers may be used for varying periods. The cast's comments may therefore vary.)

Tony: Where'd they get these acts. I thought vaudeville was dead.

John: At least it gets us away from the crap tables.

Harvey: Yeah......... My hands were starting to ice up.

John: *(He is looking at a woman at a nearby table.)* You know that woman looks familiar.............. I think I may know her...........

Tony: Wow she's a knockout.

Maria: Cool down John

(Anne slides in alongside John.....)

Anne: Yes indeed John, time to cool down.

SCENE 4

(At the crap tables Tony and Harvey are playing. Another man with a serious tremor has the dice.................He shakes the hand wildly and the dice can go anywhere.... The men are talking. John walks over)

Tony: You've gotta watch this..............The guy with the dice has some kind of tic or some disease.

(The dice go off the table.....the croupier calls a number after crawling on the floor after the dice.) (Three fingered Louie walks in)

John: I thought it's an illegal roll if the dice are off the table.

Louie: Not for this guy. He's got a thousand on every roll..........They don't want to embarrass him...... so they ignore his disability. ...How're you guys doing?? Having fun???

Tony: **Yeah!** Watching my money fly ....right to the croupier

Harvey: **C'mon   EIGHT! Baby needs a new pair of shoes.**

Tony: Not your baby........She's been out shopping for two days.

(The guy rolls again barely getting the dice on the table.)

Tony: **C'MON SEVEN**

Louie:	Hey ...You're betting the **no pass** line???. How're you gonna win if you're betting against each other?
Tony:	WIN??? .... **I'm just trying to stay even!**
John:	I couldn't sleep last night. Some lady kept bangin on my door. She created such a ruckus I finally had to let her out.
Harvey:	Yeah you and Henny Youngman.

(This goes on for a little while . At this moment Maria walks by followed by a very rigid man carrying various packages and shopping bags, who walks in lock step behind her. She walks offstage he follows.)

John:	What's with Maria??? Who's that guy following her???
Harvey:	That's her personal shopper. Three department stores chipped in to pay his salary. She also gets her own parking space.
John:	Boy that'll run into a few bucks.
Harvey:	Say Tony where's Alice...........I haven't seen her the last couple of days.
Tony:	Well it's hard to believe. She went to the exercise room. They have a treadmill there with a slot machine on it. You play while exercising.
Harvey:	Holy..................You can lose a fortune that way........You better reel that in.
Tony:	Are you kidding??? ....She's lost thirty five

pounds............She looks terrific. We made plans to come back in three months for another session.

(At this moment Doreen approaches the table and takes a place near John. He turns and sees her)

John: My God...I saw you last night ..You're Doreen Sullivan.....We knew each other in High School.

Doreen: We went to the Prom together ....Yes I remember you...................... John..........Bonham right?

John: Northside High ....Go demons..........It's been a long time. What's your name now.

Doreen: It's back to Sullivan as of three years. How about you....Are you married?

John: Yes but my wife thinks golf has a priority over Vegas. Let's have a drink and bring each other up to date. I can't believe that we could run into each other this way....................

(They walk over to a nearby table. John orders drinks.)

Doreen: I have a married daughter.. Got a divorce after her wedding..........It was brewing for a while.

John: We've been married since college. Two kids ...Boy and a girl.......grown and on their own.

Doreen: There are a lot of years and experiences under that bridge. Now I'm looking forward to restarting my life. I enjoy Vegas more than cruising.

John: Good for you. You know.........I remember that green gown you wore to the prom.   You were so proud ....like a rare flower.........

Doreen: What a lovely way to put it. .....You were pretty good looking also.....

John: Were?? Have I changed that much?

Doreen: Oh I didn't mean it that way...........You're still quite the dashing hero..............

(At this moment Anne slides in and takes a seat next to John)

Anne: Quite the dashing hero.........You must love it.

(John shrugs.)

Doreen: Is there something wrong? You seem annoyed.

John: Not at all....How could I possibly be annoyed at you.

(He slides his hand toward Doreen to touch hers and gets a poke in the ribs from Anne)

Doreen: I didn't mean to make you uncomfortable. Perhaps ....

John: I have to have dinner with my friends tonight. Can we meet ...say at eleven.............in the upstairs lounge.....for a nightcap?

Doreen: Let me see how my evening progresses   I'm having dinner at Caesars with some business associates. I may make it.

Anne: **Better make that drinks for three.**

(LIGHTS OUT)

SCENE 5

(We are in the salon of Madame Lavoisier. John enters)

Mme L: Welcome Monsieur....Are you here for a Tarot?

John: No not exactly.............I don't know if you can
help me......... My friends know of your sister in
Florida.

Mme L: Ah ..of course.............. Are you having a
problem.?..........perhaps a difficult...viagra
lack?............... I cannot help you at the
tables.............They will take away my priveleges.

John: The tables are a problem but that's not what I'm
here for.

Mme L: Please ....you can confide in me.

John: It seems so silly now.........I don't want you to
think I'm queer.............

Mme L: **Queer** I cannott fix.................**Strange** I might
manage......I was married to strange for twenty
years.

John: I'm here without my wife.................But she
shows up wherever I go. I can see and talk to her
but nobody else can. She's driving me nuts.

Mme L: Whew! For a moment there..............**I thought**

your ....you know................were shrinking.

John: God I hope not..........but I would like to do something.

Mme L: But my dear man...It is in your head and soul.........This will not leave till you return to her.

John: Isn't there anything that would help? I met a friend from high school ....and I wanted to ....review our recent past.....to update our ....friendship.

Mme L: **A cold shower three times a day would help.**

John: Well thank you anyhow..*(He gets up to leave.)*

Mme L: Here...Take this every evening.   *(She hands him a small bottle)*

John: **Aha ... a magic potion.**

Mme L: No.. a sleeping pill.........It will help to get you through the night.

(John gives her some bills which she refuses. He leaves.)

Mme L: **I will send the bill to my sister. I could have cleaned up on this one.**

(LIGHTS OUT)

SCENE 6

(In the upstairs lounge)

John: I hope she shows up......just for old times
                 sake.....

(Doreen walks in hesitatingly.....slowly approaches John's table..and sits down)

Doreen: I feel so awkward ....I don't usually have
                 drinks with married men...........I hope you don't
                 get the wrong impression.

John: Don't be silly........We're old friends ....just
                 catching up. What will you have??

(He orders two drinks)

John: Tell me about your life. You said you had a
                 business meeting? What are you into?

Doreen: I never heard it described like that before. I'm
                 designing clothes for young women. That's why
                 I'm in Vegas. I run parties with models at clubs
                 here and in LA .....to show the clothes.

John: That's fascinating. Do you have a website?

Doreen: Yes..But I wouldn't go there if I were you............
                 The clothes are ...what I would say ......mostly
                 night wear.

John: What a great idea.....Working with all those beautiful women...........but I think you would still standout............

Doreen: Why thank you kind sir..

(He starts to extend his arm slowly. Anne slides in to stand behind him with her own drink.)

Anne: I knew **you** wouldn't order one for me. ....What's with this hand holding...Aren't you kind of old for that?????

John: I didn't know you could drink also.

Doreen: But of course I can....You ordered one for me.

John: I'm sorry I didn't mean............Of course........... How do you spend your free time? I remember you were quite a dancer.

Anne: You weren't so bad yourself.

John: I didn't mean you.

Doreen: Who did you have in mind????

John: **I'm sorry**...........*(He reaches across to take her hand and Anne pokes him hard in the ribs.....He knocks the glass over on Doreen. She leaps up to wipe herself off.)*

Doreen: It looks like you started without me. ... I learned a long time that you cannot live in the past...The present is tough enough. ....Enjoy yourself in Vegas ....
Maybe we'll bump heads another time.

(She leaves)

(Anne lifts her glass high for a drink. John reaches in his pocket and takes out the vial and puts some pills in his hand and swallows them...LIGHTS OUT)

SCENE 7

(The group is back at the bus depot. Alice now has a small carry on and is much thinner. Maria has the two large suitcases.)

Harvey: Alice you look great. What happened to all your clothes??

Alice: Dumped everything.. Nothing fits...........Gave my suitcases to Maria.

Maria: The stores are great in Vegas...Especially the new Lord and Taylor. How were the crap tables?

Tony: ICY John why did you walk away from the tables? That whirling dervish threw five passes.

Harvey: We're down about 9 big ones.

John: **What are you complaining about?** You kept yelling for sevens!

Harvey: I was trying to get even.

Alice: So much for the triumphant syndicate.

Maria: I knew you'd do that.........Well that comes out of your account. I'm so upset ...I could head right back to ....Nordstoms.

Harvey: It won't happen again.

Maria: I'll see that it doesn't.

Alice: We didn't get to many fancy restaurants.

John: Yeah ...I really wanted to go to that steakhouse in Caesars.......

Tony: We spent too much time trying to get even.

Maria: You can never get even.

Harvey: Yeah ...I was down to playing the slots...looking for a jackpot.

(Louie comes onstage.)

Louie: Great trip friends. I'll stop by and see how you're doin in a few days.

John: I know you will.

(LIGHTS OUT   THEN ON)

SCENE 8

(The Petrillos enter their home. It's a mess with glasses strewn on the tables bottles of vodka and bourbon overturned, all the lights on and Minnie wearing a blond wig is asleep on the sofa.)

Alice: **Oh my God!** What happened????? Ma wake up...... Are you all right.

Tony: All right??? She's **polluted...........**

Minnie: *(awakening)* Hey you back already???? Where is everybody?

Tony: Who's everybody??? You been partying?

Minnie: All my friends.

Alice: What friends??? You haven't spoken to anyone in six years. It smells like a barroom in here. Have you been smoking??

Minnie: **That's how much you notice.** I got a lot of friends. They're in assisted living........................... I just assisted their living a little more............ We had a little gathering last night.

Alice: A gathering ....you mean a blowout!

Tony: How long you been boozing ...on my Booze??

Minnie: Oh cut it out. I thought it was covered in the rent!........Where's Edward??....Eddie?..........Eddie?

(At this moment a disheviled man crawls out from behind the couch and runs offstage)

Alice: **Mom I think your in store for a big rise in rent.**

(LIGHTS OUT THEN ON)

SCENE 9

(We're in the Bonham's home. John walks in.)

John: Hi...Anybody home?? ....I'm back.

(Anne walks in. She has a suitcase.)

John: Hi Annie. How did the golf go???

Anne: I won....... Fantastic game. I had 23 putts in the last round.

John: Why that's marvelous. You're pro material.............What's with the suitcase?

Anne: Oh I never had a chance to tell you............I got a call from Tommy Greene........They're having sort of a college reunion. I decided to go.

John: You mean the Tom Greene you used to go with. He must be old and fat by now.

Anne: Probably..................He just ran the Boston Marathon...............Oh there's my taxi...Have to run.

John: How long will you be away?

Anne: About a week.

John: But where can I reach you??? Where will you be??

(As she leaves the stage)

Anne: **Las Vegas baby....Las Vegas**

               END   **LIGHTS OUT**

IT'S A LIVING

A NEW ORIGINAL PLAY

BY

BERNARD GARDNER

Cast in order of appearance:

Lillie Harte
Ellie Weingarten
Clerk
Baron von Horsch
Franz Rohrbach
Herb Weingarten
Camilla
Edvard
(people at the club)
Thomas Harte
Eddie Harte
Samantha Harte
Three Patients
Preacher(non speaking)
Other son and daughter-in-law and their children (non speaking)

(The play is set in the present.)

ACT I
Scene 1

(Set in a senior daycare facility. The facility has a small entrance with a desk and a clerk. Lilly and Ellie enter and approach the intake clerk. To the left is the lounge area with several people sitting and talking. It occupies the major portion of the stage. It is fitted with couch , some card tables and a large TV set.. A large open doorway separates the areas.)

Lilly: Hi. My parents are preregistered for daytime care, including lunch. My mother will be by herself today. I will pick her up late this afternoon.

Clerk: Yes indeed. Hi Mrs. Weingarten. Welcome back. The other ladies are already at lunch. *(to Lillie)* You know you must be back by 5 PM. The office will close promptly at five and the other ladies will be gone by that time.

Lillie: I will do my best. I have several errands after work. Just leave her in the lounge. She'll be fine.

(Lillie leaves)

(It is later .6PM....As evening approaches Ellie Weingarten is sitting in the empty lounge when Baron von Horsch enters.)

Ellie: Well hello there. I didn't know there were other people here. I'm Ellie Weingarten.

Baron: Ah..yes .....There are several of us..........I mean others. We have an arrangement for assisted living..... Baron von Horsch at your service.

Ellie: Why that's wonderful..... This huge facility would be such a waste being used just for day care.................Do they have many activities for the guests??

Baron: Yes. They have this large lounge for TV ...although most of us have TVs in our quarters. They show movies ...usually Karloff, Lugosi and Chaney....We love the old..............horror shows.

Ellie: I used to see them every Saturday.............when I was a kid I mean. Do they serve good dinners? The lunches they prepare are excellent.

Baron: Well most of us don't eat very much. Not much appetite.....But are you hungry? I'm sure I can get the kitchen to put something together.

Ellie: Oh no,. my daughter should be here any minute.........She's picking me up after work. She had to take my husband to the doctor today. We live with my daughter and her family............two grandchildren. How long have you been here? You don't seem disabled.

Baron: Oh most of us do have a ...disability. Two grandchildren.... must be a bit hectic.

(Rohrbach enters the room. He approaches the Baron.)

Baron: Oh do meet Franz Rohrbach one my dearest friends. Franz this is Ellie Weingarten. She.... well ..... what is it you do here?

(Rohrbach walks to Ellie, takes her hand and kisses it)

Rohrbach: My pleasure.................Yes............we seldom have visitors................

Ellie: Oh I'm not a visitor............. We're in the senior day care program. My daughter should be here momentarily. She's not usually this late.

Baron: Don't apologize......we're delighted to meet you.

Ellie: You are so well dressed. Is it very formal here? ...Do you dress for dinner every night?

Rohrbach: Oh no............ Actually it is usually quite informal. ....And most of us have already............eaten. But we tend to be out............on the town most evenings.

Ellie: Doesn't sound like you need assisted living.

Rohrbach: It's not exactly wild activity. The Baron here runs a small club in town and we occasionally provide some entertainment. Don't worry we retire well before daybreak.

Ellie: You both have such interesting names. Are you foreign?

Baron: Foreign born perhaps. ....But we are all American citizens. My title stems from my homeland in upper Silesia, ... the Grand Duchy of Moravia in the tenth century.

Ellie: That's wonderful ....You can trace your family back so far.

Baron: Yes............My family.........

Rohrbach: I believe your daughter has arrived. Such a pleasure to meet you.

(Ellie leaves the lounge to meet her daughter, Lilly walks into the room slightly out of breath)

Lilly: I rushed all the way....I knew the others would

have left by now, including the manager. Daddy is ok.........I left him at home.

Ellie: Oh I was fine. I met these lovely gentlemen.............

Lilly: Why that's wonderful. I thought everyone would be gone by now. . I didn't realize that the facility was used at night.

Ellie: Apparently they use the facility as an assisted living home. Although the gentlemen I met seemed pretty healthy.. ...Now where did they go.?

Lilly: Fascinating............How many occupants are there?

Ellie: Seems like at least four. I'm sure they'll be around another time and I'll introduce you.

Lillie: That will be a great pleasure.

Scene 2

(In their room at Lillie's home. Ellie and Herb are discussing the day's activities) (The room is large, it is set with a double bed and a sofa facing a large TV sitting atop a dresser with three large drawers. There is a table in front of the sofa. Alongside the TV is a small desk and chair. Near the entrance is a half refrigerator with a small microwave on it. A long closet sits opposite the refrigerator. The room has been an addition to the house. A bathroom , not seen, is outside near the entrance.)

Ellie: What did he say?...............

Herb: It's spread...........Shit news! ....He wants to start chemo.......... but it won't work...........I looked it up.

Ellie: But it's a slow grower.... You've got a lot more time than I have.

Herb: **I don't want any time without you.** ....Fifty eight years .... I don't know a world without you. I don't want to.

Ellie: Stop the dramatic crap...... you'll be fine....Think of the kids....You'll meet other people.

Herb: The kids??? They've got their own lives. They don't need an old fart hanging around. ....I love you.....I've always loved only you. That's a lot of cheating I passed up.

Ellie: What makes you so sure you were the only one.

Herb: How the hell did we make it all these years.

Ellie: Easy.........You were always working while I managed everyone's life. Not much time left over for fighting. Although, I admit, there were times I could have slugged you.

Herb: You're right. That's the key to a long marriage. Develop other interests and don't dote on the day to day annoyances.

Ellie: It helps to have the finances, but you're right ....today's marriage failures are often due to over analysis, too much bickering.

Herb: You're still beautiful ....just like when we met.........I'm old and ragged ...I don't deserve a knockout like you.

Ellie: Your eyesight has deteriorated............Maybe you need a repeat on the cataract operation. Although I admit we certainly argue less and less these past few years.

Herb: A pleasure of old age..............After a few minutes you can't remember what you were mad about.

Ellie: The kids............all of them divorced. Not one of them learned a thing about marriage by watching us. Did we do something wrong?

Herb: Stop with the blame!.. Today the first marriage is a tryout.......Easy come Easy go....It's all on a signed piece of paper...You don't like something just tear it up........ The second marriage, however,..... carries a sense of panic. If that doesn't work out..............

Ellie: Did we ever think of divorce?

Herb: Never!........It wasn't ever an option. We worked it out ...and then forgot about it. More important things to do.

Ellie: I made a lot of decisions without consulting you......

Herb: Thank God. I had enough on my mind .... But we did agree on where we wanted to live and bring up the kids and luckily that worked out well for us. How was your day at the center?

Ellie: Our card group didn't show today......I'm having trouble concentrating anyhow. I don't think I can play much longer...........But something interesting happened .... In the evening two gentlemen came in. Apparently they have a night residence in the facility...............Strange.........I never saw them during the day before..........must be working , I guess.

Herb: Gentlemen??

Ellie: Yes. Foreign born I would say..............one's a Baron. There are four living at that place. They say it's quite nice.

Herb: Really.........I thought the help all left at five.

Ellie: No. The baron offered me a sandwich and said the kitchen was functioning. Come with me tomorrow. I'll ask Lillie to pick us up late.

Herb: Ok with me. Maybe we can have a bite with these guys.

Scene 3

(At the facility, Herb and Ellie are in the lounge when Baron and Rohrbach enter.)

Baron: Why how nice to see you again, Ellie. And you brought your husband.

Ellie: Yes...This is Herb...........The baron and Mr. Rohrbach.

Rohrbach: Oh please...Franz.........A pleasure to meet you. May I get you something from the kitchen? A sandwich ?.........I believe we have some meat left over from last night which should be delicious.

Herb: No. Thank you very much. Our daughter will be picking us up soon. Ellie was very impressed meeting you yesterday. So I thought I would trail along today.

Baron: And what did you do before retirement, Herb

Herb: I was a research biologist for a major pharmaceutical firm.

Rohrbach: Of course! I have read some of your papers......... on cellular DNA malformations in cancer cells....I have an interest in DNA myself. But I have never published anything.

(Camilla and Edvard enter casually.)

Baron: Oh the four of us are here.........May I introduce
                   Camilla and Edvard former Prince ....I mean
                   descended from the royal family in Lichtenstein....
                   These are Herb and Ellie Weingarten.

Camilla: Charmed..........

*(She extends her hand to Herb and nods to Ellie. Edvard bows to Herb and
takes Ellie's hand to kiss it. Ellie shudders)*

Edvard: Oh I am so sorry. I was just having an iced drink
                   in the dining room.

Herb: And how do you folks spend your days?

Baron: Resting mostly.........We are all retired now...But
                   we are up pretty late at night..............You might
                   say we are night owls...

Herb: Extraordinary.

Rohrbach: But I have a spectacular suggestion....We are all
                   going to Baron's club this evening. Why not join
                   us. Call your daughter...........I will see to it that
                   you get home safely.

Ellie: I am hardly dressed for night clubbing.

Edvard: Nonsense. It is a very informal club. Camilla is
                   singing tonight.

(Herb takes out a cell phone and talks silently into it)

Herb: I think we'll take you up on this.

Baron: Excellent! Rohrbach will drive you. We
                   three will use our own transportation.

Scene 4

(At the club. The club is an intimate night spot with a small stage and a piano player. Several tables are scattered about with a few couples eating and drinking.)

(Herb, Ellie and Rohrbach arrive and move toward a small table already occupied by Baron, Edvard and Camilla. They have a tray of snacks and a bottle of wine and glasses.)

Herb:	My heavens I can't believe you beat us here.....You must have flown!
Rohrbach:	Well they went on a more direct route. Sorry for the delay.
Ellie:	Oh don't apologize Herb was just being cute. What an interesting place. Do you come here often??
Camilla:	Oh yes...The Baron owns it .... You might say it's our own little haunt...We have different entertainers from evening to evening. Tonight will be my turn.
Edvard:	Yes she has a lovely voice. She has sung at many Halls in many countries over the years. You're in for a treat.

(Camilla rises and reaches the stage and confers with the pianist. Scattered applause at the prospect)

Herb:	She hardly looks old enough to have so much experience.
Edvard:	Old enough..........Why she's over............
Baron:	Thirty............We won't divulge her real age......... Edvard!
Edvard:	No of course........No lady would tolerate that.

(As Camilla begins to sing "All I want from you" from "Phantom" several men bring their chairs close to the stage and show fascination with her.)

Ellie:	A beautiful voice...and look at those men.......Why she's a real Vamp.
Rohrbach:	*(anxiously)* **Why do you use that word?**
Ellie:	Sorry ..just an expression...........It's the way she attracted all that male attention.
Herb:	Tell me Franz, have you done research in this field....
Rohrbach:	Not personally....The instrumentation has passed me by. I became interested during a stay in England by association with the great scientists who first described rejection and chimerism...........through their papers of course.
Herb:	We have come a long way since that time. Fortunately the surgeons forged ahead with transplantation at a time when no one thought it possible.
Rohrbach:	Yes and now they work at the sub-cellular level. It would soon be possible to isolate the genetic stimulus to cancer growth.
Herb:	Too late for Ellie and me I'm afraid.

Rohrbach: Oh I'm sorry to hear that. Please have something to eat...I'll order some more drinks.

Herb: These snacks are delicious. Can I get some garlic powder for the tomato sauce??

Baron: Our chef never uses it! Excuse me I must circulate...Enjoy yourselves. Franz will see to it that you are driven home safely.

Herb: Thank you for your hospitality. Perhaps we could take that more direct route.

Scene 5

(Herb and Ellie are in their quarters later that evening)

Ellie: Well I feel safe again.

Lillie: Glad you're ok. Did you want something to eat, I can put something together downstairs.

Herb: No Thanks honey, Neither of us is very hungry..

(Lillie leaves)

Herb: She knows about the doctor's report. I don't want to deteriorate in front of her and the kids.

Ellie: You won't. They'll put us in hospice before that happens.

Herb: It won't change anything...........Look we still

169

have some money left over from the sale of the house. I'm not spending it on chemotherapy that our insurance won't cover....................I always promised myself that I would leave something for Joe and Lillie.

Ellie: We thought your pension from the company would hold up.

Herb: Well it hasn't...............And their health insurance is a piece of crap.................. I can't stand living with Ellie and the Nazi.............. They have their own lives.

Ellie: They don't mind as much as you think.......... and the kids love us. It was the same with your parents.............

Herb: We were supposed to be better off. What happened?

Ellie: We were better off..........We just had a few setbacks.

Herb: We had a good life. Traveled ....Made good love...........

Ellie: Speak for yourself old man..............Stop sounding like it's all over. We'll have a few good years left.

Herb: Not for me...........and I've seen you gasping at night...I can't stand trying to figure who's gonna go first. I can tell you if it's you ...you can expect me right on your tail......................

(Herb reaches over and they kiss.)

Herb: I love feeling you up.

Ellie: I enjoy it also.

Herb: I can't even play a little ball with the kids.

Ellie: I know ......I'm starting to forget the endings to some of the fairy tails

Herb: Happily ever after usually suffices..............What did you think of those creepy people last night.

Ellie: **I think they are all Vampires!**

Herb: Oh please Ellie be serious.

Ellie: No I mean it.   Did you feel that
Edvard's hand..........It was ice cold.......
no life to it...............And their night time
appearances...........And they almost jumped when
I said that Camilla was vamping those men.

Herb: It certainly is strange..........but that's
nonsense.........they made no attempt to attack us.
....

Ellie: .... and how did they arrive at the club
so fast???

Herb: I actually felt safe around them. They seem to lead an interesting life.....although it's mostly at night.............They don't seem to have any disabilities.

Ellie: What the hell are you thinking about, now.

Herb: I don't believe they're vampires............that's a fantasy........but they are strange.............Maybe they have a suggestion to relieve my back pain.

Ellie: Oh Herb ..You didn't say anything.

Herb: I wouldn't burden you.............I got a prescription ....

Ellie: Oh I'm so sorry.........

Herb: I knew it would affect you this way..........Let's go back tomorrow and see these people and find out what's fact and what's fiction.

Ellie: I know you have something in mind.

Act II
Scene 1

(At the breakfast table. Herb is eating while Ellie is serving coffee. Lillie is washing some dishes and the two children Eddie and Samantha are having cereal. Tom is reading the newspaper.)

Tom: Look at this.........They're extending unemployment payments again. These people would never have to look for a job.

Herb: Tommy there are five applicants for every available job. You can't let people starve.

Lillie: Don't start again. I'm not going through this..... Especially in front of the kids.

Tom: Ok, ok...........I don't want my kids to starve either...........we'll get some republican relief soon.

Ellie: Herb Be quiet and eat your eggs. Anyone for more coffee?

Eddie: Grandpa can we go down to the baseball field and watch a game.?

Herb: I don't think I can quite manage it today Eddie. *(He turns to Lillie)* I'm sorry I'm not doing my grandfatherly duties. There are perverts all over the neighborhood. I couldn't cope if someone grabbed one of the kids. I can't move fast anymore.

Tom: Most of the perverts are playing in the game .... They should be out looking for a job.

Herb:	The ministry is pretty well filled now!
Tom:	Now............
Ellie:	*(interrupting)* What's the matter with you two....... Politics isn't enough now you have to bring religion into it............**How about gay rights and abortion let's really get into it.**
Herb:	All right, all right ....I'll quit.

(Herb rises and pushes back his chair, taking a few missteps backwards, catching himself.)

Herb:	I'm going to sit on the porch a while.
Tom:	Here take the paper. It's the Wall Street Journal...........Just stay off the editorial page, you might get sick. *(He passes the paper to Herb)*
Sam:	Grandpa will you read to me ?
Herb:	Sure ...c'mon outside. I'll use the paper ..I know you like fairy tales.

(They both exit. Tom goes off in a different direction. The women are cleaning up.)

Ellie:	I'm sorry Lil.
Lillie:	Don't apologize. Dad's not doing so well is he?
Ellie:	We're both sort of falling apart...............Don't look so down in the mouth. ....It's bound to get that way...
Lillie:	I don't mean to get depressed. Are you having pain?

Ellie: We've thought about Hospice..... Herb wants to look into other options........like that assisted care facility you take us to each day. The people we met there seem to be doing okay.

Lillie: I'd like to meet them.

Ellie: That may not be such a great idea right now. No I don't think so.

Scene 2

(We are back at the facility. Baron and Rohrbach are talking.)

Baron: Frantz what is this new club you are applying for.

Rohrbach: It is a very private club. If you passed the building on the street you couldn't know it contained one of the most exclusive clubs in the city.

Baron: Really...............

Rohrbach: Yes the membership are some of the wealthiest men in New York. They have the option of eating at the most exclusive restaurants in the world, but being exhausted by the fancy sauces and dishes they have each evening they retire here to enjoy the food they really love.

Baron: Amazing. What is the menu like??

Rohrbach: Well they have a special of franks and beans, and many evenings they serve peanut butter and jelly sandwiches, and one fellow often has cream cheese and lox on a toasted bagel..............says it reminds him of a girl he knew in college.

Baron: I see... Is he Jewish.??

Rohrbach: Hardly. They let one Jewish fellow in so they pass the anti-discrimination laws in the city. He's a banker who made a fortune in foreign currency. ..They figured he'd have no one to converse with anyhow............................ No women however.

They had one who wore dresses with very low cut necklines. She was dismissed when she bent forward and a senior member spilled a snifter of 75 year old brandy over his pants.

Baron: What do you do besides eat?

Rohrbach: Interesting... After dinner they bring out this huge board...sort of like a monopoly board which they sit around......and they throw dice...except all the properties are real. They may buy or sell some of them. One fellow went bankrupt on a vacation property owned by the B&O railway. The club senior had warned him that you couldn't build hotels on the railways.................... but they got together and bailed him out.

Baron: I suppose you get some information on hot investments

Rohrbach: Yes I've done well.

(Edvard and Camiila walk in. They are having a serious discussion.)

Edvard: I can't believe you would do this. You hardly know this fellow.

Camilla: He's such an adoring young man. He is very romantic and gallant. I am attracted to him.

Edvard: I can see......But, of course, you must be cognizant of the difference in your ages.........

Camilla: Please ....It's not the first time a lady took pleasure in the company of a younger man.................

Edvard: **But seven hundred years??????????????**

Camilla: *(with a flare of her hands)...POOF*

(They nod to the others)

Baron: What do you make of these people from last night?

Rohrbach: They know...............We have been too friendly with them.........

Camilla: We must be careful.

Edvard: They are quite pleasant..........they won't say anything....I like them.

Rohrbach: Yes I would look forward to discussing some scientific topics with Herb.

Baron: Now in our present condition we can have some friends.

(Ellie and Herb arrive. They walk in apprehensively and sit down)

Baron: Have you eaten? Can I get you anything? A drink perhaps?

Herb: I don't suppose you'd have a bloody Mary?

Ellie: **Stop Herb.** That's not funny....................Herb and I have been a little anxious about some of your ....activities.

Rohrbach: Look it's no use hiding anymore. ....I will tell you in strictest confidence.

Herb: Please. We're not here to threaten your exposure or play around with wooden stakes.   .... I wouldn't even know where to start.........I'm not van Helsing or anything. Besides you could have attacked us at any time............

Ellie: Yes why didn't you??

Camilla:	There's no need for us to do that anymore.
Edvard:	We have made adjustments. Our group is............. you might say....**Born again Vampires.**
Baron:	Let me explain. We are all citizens of the United States. We have made arrangements with some friends to allow us to stay here. We no longer have the constant thirst for blood.
Rohrbach:	Yes....A doctor friend has diagnosed us with various marrow dystrophies which require a daily transfusion.
Baron:	It is all set up for us. When we awaken we go to a treatment room for our blood transfusions. The local blood bank supplies their outdated units which are fine for us and that restores our strength.
Camilla:	**And it's all covered by medicare!**
Ellie:	Amazing.............You hardly look old enough for medicare
Edvard:	Camilla is over seven hundred years old.
Herb:	**My God!**
Edvard:	If you don't mind we prefer not to use that language.
Herb:	Sorry................What a terrific system. Is everything we've heard about Vampires true?? ....You can make new ones?
Ellie:	Herb please. ....
Herb:	And you can live forever?

Baron:	It is not quite as pleasant as you may think. For example Edvard almost mutilated his face recently...............He tried to trim his beard.
Herb:	Why would that be such a problem?
Edvard:	**Have you ever shaved without a mirror?????????????**
Camilla:	Yes and I had a terrific toothache several months ago. Do you think you can find a dentist with night hours.
Rohrbach:	And you constantly have to watch your diet. We cannot eat Italian food.
Herb:	Yes I suppose the garlic............
Baron:	Would make us very ill. ....and Rohrbach cannot fly anymore.
Ellie:	Why? Is that why he drove the other night?
Rohrbach:	Yes. I have become somewhat hard of hearing. I keep bumping into buildings.
Herb:	But you can't die................can you? You have no fatal diseases?
Baron:	**Sometimes I wish......................**
Camilla:	Don't be so over dramatic! We have our little pleasantries. **It's a living.**
Edvard:	Yes ...as though we have much of a choice.
Herb:	But don't the little Buffys come running around looking for you.

Rohrbach:	They'd never think to look in an assisted living facility. That's why we need to keep a low profile.
Baron:	Besides we don't bother anyone anymore.
Ellie:	**But there must be more of you!**
Camilla:	No not really many. We have some branches in Europe. But every civilized country has full medical benefits so as long as we maintain citizenship we're covered. I suppose some day a busy body reporter might uncover something But we'll just move on and he will end up under psychiatric treatment.
Ellie:	I don't understand these ailments you complain of............Aren't you supposed to be healthy...........I mean if you live forever.
Rohrbach:	Well we have our little warts and blemishes............but nothing fatal.
Herb:	That's the part that interests me.
Camilla:	Life is not all roses, as you say, even for us. But at least we no longer need to thirst..............well you know!
Herb:	Ellie and I are not that fortunate. We are near the end of our run. Neither of us wants to be separated from the other.
Ellie:	Our lives have been entwined for so long ....we pretty much depend on each other. Besides we are becoming a true burden on our children.
Edvard:	But don't your children have something to say?
Ellie:	They would be torn by guilt for any decision they made. I would like ....We would like to spare

them that. My mother died of cancer and seeing her deteriorate left me with guilt and regrets.

Baron: But today they have Hospice care ,,,,,,,,,,,,you would die in peace and without pain.

Herb: We have thought of that, and would choose that soon enough. But now you've opened another possibility. We could live forever together.

Baron: NO!

Herb: Why not? ...It makes excellent sense to us.

Rohrbach: Please Herb you do not know what you are asking. Let us talk it over. Come back when you are ready for an answer.

Herb: Time is.............

Camilla: *(interrupting)* Consider...............you are asking to enter a universe **where there is no time.**

Scene 3

(This scene depicts the interrogation of Hospice patients by Herb. It is staged as a clinical setting with three patients and Herb. One patient is in a bed with an IV and two are in reclining chairs, one having his lunch on a tray. Herb is sitting in a chair to the stage right and the others in a semi-circle to the left facing the audience.)

Herb: I appreciate your willingness to talk to me. I may be entering this facility with my wife shortly.

Patient 1: That's tough. The food's ok , if you can eat......... the nurses are friendly and there are plenty of meds if you need them.

Herb: What's going through your mind? How do you spend your time.

Patient 2: *(In the bed)* That's a stupid question! Thinking about the next injection of pain meds.

Patient 1: Or the food. Hoping we get the tray early.

Patient 3: Or what's on television.

Herb: Do you dwell much on your past?

Patient 1: The past can be a horror or a comfort. Memories are all we have. Hopes and ambitions are for others.

Herb:	Does the prospect of death depress or frighten you?
Patient 2:	**I'm waiting for it with open arms.** That stupid angel is running around the world killing young people and decent people while I lie here trapped in this bed.
Patient 3:	If you're depressed or frightened they have a pill for that. It's better not thinking about it.
Patient 1:	The one pill they won't give you is the one for permanent peace. ....unless you're having a really bad time. Then they speed up the IV.
Herb:	But don't you look forward to these last moments with your loved ones?
Patient1:	It relieves their guilt! Otherwise why would I enjoy contemplating what I'm leaving behind. Both they and I would be better off without the visits. It's a chore for all of us.
Patient 2:	I agree. What's the sense of having them see me like this? Do I need to have my grandchildren see me like this???
Herb:	If you could live forever would you grasp that chance?
Patient 3:	I have lots of money. I tried everything to survive. I bribed the doctors to find me organs to help me survive. Nothing worked. I could enjoy more years...Living forever would free me of all bonds......I would never care about the consequences of anything I did.
Patient 2:	Live??? In what condition?? With pain or without pain.

Herb: Without pain.

Patient 2: **You think physical pain is the only torment?** Is your life so wonderful?

 Does the no-pain formula include those you love? Or does watching their trials pump you up?

Herb: Suppose you could be with the one you love. ....Forever...............

Patient 1: Show me the guarantees. I want to see the contract before I sign up.

Patient 3: I accept............Provided I could access my bank account...............and the kids haven't spent it all before this takes effect.

Herb: So the key is immensely personal and what guarantees would you want.

Patient 3: Easy!.... no diseases

Patient 2: I would need a lot more.I would just spend more years worrying about my family.

Patient 1: My life was not so perfect either...............and my family would never know, of course, which means I would have to get on without them or watch them die. That might not seem so pleasant. ..Besides ..I'm not such a hotshot on the computer now ....How would I manage a hundred years from now.

Patient 2: Forever seems so long..............

(Herb steps away and Ellie enters . They hug and have a discussion away from the patients)

Herb: I have thought about it ...but I can't decide. So many questions come up.

Ellie: I know........We really don't know what it would be like...........or if we would be the same............I love you but we probably won't have the same lives.

Herb: The prospect thrills me, however. Perhaps it would be best to let others decide......those who know.

Scene 4

(Months later) (Herb and Ellie are lying side by side on a bier. A spotlight illuminates them but the room is darkened. A small light is cast on the front of the stage where the Vampires are gathered.)

Rohrbach: Let's do it....Let's help them. We have the power...

Edvard: Yes, I like them. It will be different.

Camilla: They do not understand. They will regret the decision.

Edvard: You are just unhappy without the trappings and attention you got as princess.

Camilla: You forget what a life I led then. I was feared and detested constantly hounded............. This chance to leave that behind, as long as it lasts, is very welcome.

Baron: We are not even certain what form they will take. They may decide to forego the transfusions and revert to the old ways.

Rohrbach: We will guide them. They will become part of our group.

Camilla: No ...I agree with the Baron. They are basing a decision on incomplete data.
          (To Rohrbach) Surely you as a scientist would recognize this as folly.

187

Rohrbach: You are certainly correct. Yes it may not turn out as they think. Our psyches are attuned to our lack of emotion and personal involvement. We only strive to avoid loss of strength. There are no guarantees.

Baron: **I too have enjoyed their company. They are at peace now. I will not subject them to the tyranny of immortality.**

(They quietly leave. The lights dim. When the spotlight goes on to the bier there are now two coffins side by side. A preacher is a black suit is silently reading from a book. The family consisting of Lilly and Tommy, their two children Joe and his wife and children, file slowly and silently in and stand facing the coffins. One of Lilly's children buries her head in Lilly's thigh and the lights go out)

END